AF102553

HIGHTOWER III
THE RECKONING

GoTo Publish

HIGHTOWER III
THE RECKONING

D.F. SPARKS

Hightower III
The Reckoning
Copyright © 2020 by D. F. Sparks

Library of Congress Control Number: 2019918728
ISBN-13:   Paperback: 978-1-64749-001-0
           ePub: 978-1-64749-002-7

All rights reserved. No part of this publication may be reproduced, distributed, or transmitted in any form or by any means, including photocopying, recording, or other electronic or mechanical methods, without the prior written permission of the publisher or author, except in the case of brief quotations embodied in critical reviews and certain other noncommercial uses permitted by copyright law.

Although every precaution has been taken to verify the accuracy of the information contained herein, the author and publisher assume no responsibility for any errors or omissions. No liability is assumed for damages that may result from the use of information contained within.

Printed in the United States of America

GoToPublish LLC
1-888-337-1724
www.gotopublish.com
info@gotopublish.com

Contents

Prelude vii
Chapter 1 1
Chapter 2 17
Chapter 3 31
Chapter 4 49
Chapter 5 65
Chapter 6 79
Chapter 7 95
Chapter 8 111

Prelude

It had been over a year since the fire at the ranch, just West of Las Cruces, New Mexico had taken the lives of Elizabeth Carter and her complete gang. And during that year twins had been born to Hightower and his wife Rachel. It had been an uneventful year. So Hightower had spent most of his time building new buildings, corral's and fencing in his pastures to contain his cattle. When he wasn't doing that he was setting on the front porch with his two children and the two border Collie's, who had been trained to protect them.

It was on the day when there was a small amount of work to be done so as usual. Hightower was on the front porch with the twins when a lone rider came riding up the lane leading up to the main ranch house. The man wore a flat brimmed black hat and he rode a buckskin horse. He was also draped in a black slicker being that it had been raining for the better part of three days, but Hightower could not understand what would bring a visit from this certain gentlemen.

The gentlemen was Wade Jackson United States marshal, and from the look on his face. He was not bringing good news. When he pulled up at the front porch, he didn't bother getting down from his buckskin, he simply said, "Edward, when the Las Cruces Sheriff went through the ashes of the burned out ranch house where the Carter gang made their last stand. There was no sign of Elizabeth Carter. What they did find was a tunnel that had been erected in the basement that went for some 100 yards, and came out below the horizon and there were tracks that proved two people had escaped. It has been said that Elizabeth Carter has been seen at a place called Red Stone Arizona, but when the Marshall's arrived there, she was long gone. Not long after that, another gang started robbing banks and the thing that scares the hell out of everybody is that gang is being led a woman who cares nothing about killing innocent people. We believe it's Elizabeth Carter and I have been directed to give you these orders from the Atty. Gen, his orders to you are, bring her in DEAD OR ALIVE"!!!

Chapter 1

The train ride from Las Cruces New Mexico to Lake Charles, Louisiana was a long and anxious trip for both Hightower and Comanche, but for the first time in almost 3 months. Hightower was able to sleep without the face of Elizabeth Carter popping up his dreams. Even Comanche seemed to be a lot more at ease, Hightower was at the point where he was believing that Comanche was starting to enjoy riding on a train. The closer that Hightower got to Lake Charles, the more anxious he got. Rachel had given birth to twins, and they were almost a month and a half old and he had never seen them.

The Porter on the train that Hightower had paid to keep an eye on Comanche had started to get quite attached to the big gray stallion and it seemed that feeling was mutual. There was a special trip made back to the stock car at least three times a day to make sure that the stallion had all he wanted to eat or drink, and he was brushed down in the evening every day, and it seemed that the stallion was becoming to expect to be brushed.

As Hightower had made up his mind that when he did get home. It was going to be a long time before he ever left again. There was something about knowing that you had become a father and that there was a very beautiful woman waiting for your return, and he never thought he would say it, but he missed married life, he missed Rachel and he yearned to see his children for the first time. Rachel had named her son, Edward Hightower Junior, and the little girl had been named Rebecca Marie Hightower. There had been a lot of tension and worry about Rachel carrying the babies to full term because of her bullet wound suffered at the hands of Elizabeth Carter's stepson. But evidently a lot of worrying had been in vain, because Rachel gave birth to both children in less than an hour and a half after going into labor.

She had spent a lot of her time along with Dorothy, training, two border Collie pups to guard the children. It seemed that both puppies had been very easily trained because each puppy slept beside each crib. Rachel had never told Hightower what she had named the dogs, but he figured it would be something, right out of left field and probably after a very famous partnership like Lewis and Clarke, or it could be after a president and vice president. Hightower said a silent prayer that the dogs would not be named after any politician, these dogs need to be able to be counted on all the time, which is something that you cannot say about politicians at any level.

The only thing that Hightower wished he had of done, was to of stayed around and checked the remains of the ranch house that burned and got a head count of the people that died in the fire, especially to satisfy his mind that Elizabeth Carter existed no more, but he had been in a big rush to get back home, so he had ask the Sheriff of Las Cruces to check it out for him and let him know what he found. The crazy laugh that he heard from Elizabeth Carter right before the gunshot still echoed in Hightower's mind.

As the train pulled in to Lake Charles. It didn't take Hightower long to have the big gray stallion off of the train and he was preparing to saddle him, when a voice came from behind him, saying, "Edward Hightower, it's about time you got home. "Turning around he was surprised to find not only Rachel, but Dorothy, judge Tatum and of course his wife Amy all standing there with big smiles on their faces. Rachel was carrying Edward Hightower Junior, and Dorothy was caring his daughter Rebecca Marie Hightower, as he stood looking at the family. He felt a pride swell up in his chest. Knowing that he finally once again had roots and a family that loved him. He in turn would love and protect each person standing there in front of him till his last dying breath.

Rachel handed his son to him, and at the same time, Dorothy placed Rebecca in the cradle of his other arm. SO there he stood, with two babies snuggled into the cradle of each arm, and laying peacefully against his chest.

Both babies looked as peaceful as they were both asleep and had not open their eyes, even for a moment. He looked at Rachel and ask, "Are they always this good or is this the calm before the storm." Rachel smiled and with a girlish giggle she said, "they are awfully good babies, but every now and then they have their little spells of crying, but mostly they marvel at the two dogs and pull their hair. I really don't know what I would have done without mom and Dorothy's help, I was pretty weak after giving birth." Then Dorothy reached and got Rebecca and Amy took Junior as Rachel put her arms around Edward's neck. She whispered in his ear, "I was so worried about you, I feared every day that you would be hurt or worse, but you're here now and if I have anything to say about it, you're not going to leave again, at least not anytime soon."

Hightower felt a tap on his shoulder and when he turned around, it was the judge. With a worried look on his face he asked, "Is it really over, Edward? Is Elizabeth Carter dead?" Studying for just a few moments before answering Hightower finally said, "I seen her go into the ranch house, I stood and watched that house burn to the ground, but as for actually seeing Elizabeth's body, I didn't actually see her body in the ashes, but the Sheriff of Las Cruces will be going through the ashes when it cools and is going to send me a report on what he finds. As far as I could tell, no one got out of that house alive, but to actually say that Elizabeth Carter is dead I have no proof of that at this day and time."

In the meantime, Rachel and the rest of the family had gotten back aboard the buckboard and Rachel said, "Let's go home. Edward, there will be plenty of time to catch up and to ask and answer questions when we get home."

As Hightower turned and prepared to mount the big gray, the judge smiled real big and said, "Welcome to married life Edward, you have most certainly just been given your first set of orders by your wife." Then he slapped Hightower on the back and laughed. In response Hightower simply said, "I reckon so judge, I reckon so. But I really don't mind at all.

The buckboard pulled away with the judge driving and Hightower bringing up the rear. It would take an hour, give or take a few minutes to get to the ranch. So Hightower took his time and got reacquainted with the scenery and the sounds of birds and the chatter of squirrels, to him it was as if someone was orchestrating a symphony what was being played by the animals and he felt a peace that he hadn't felt in three or four months, then he thought to himself, Thank you Lord, for bringing me back home. "For the rest of the trip back to the ranch, Hightower studied each tree, and each small stream that fed into the Creek that eventually fed into the small bay where all the fishing boats took shelter in storms. He noticed each and every small grassy area where he and Rachel used to picnic or just go for walks. When they got to the place where the stream emptied out into the Creek that flowed by his ranch house, there was a very large, and very deep swimming hole where he remembered taking Rachel and Dorothy, along with trooper Mason for a picnic and an afternoon of frolicking in the swimming hole and just enjoy in life. Hightower had not even noticed that he had stopped Comanche, and they both were just standing and staring at the spot where the romance with Rachel had began. It was only when Rachel called his name that he jolted back to reality. All Hightower could think of to say was, "yes, dear, I'll be right with you."

When they crossed the small bridge Hightower turned loose of the reins because there was no doubt in his mind that Comanche knew his way home, what he wasn't prepared for was Comanche, breaking into a run. It was as if the stallion was glad to be home again, so Hightower just let him run.

As they entered the barn yard they were met by what seemed to be a whole platoon of troopers, one sergeant, one Cpl., and one two star general. The first thing the general asked was where was Andrews, Lewis, and Mason.?

Hightower, dismounted and started loosening the cinch on Comanches saddle and with a smirk on his face he said to the general, "well, Howdy to you to general, I figured they knew their way back here. Besides they had to gather up all of their gear and saddle their horses and sign the paperwork so that the railroad could get paid for transporting the three troopers. And I gave them permission Sir, to stop by the nearest saloon and drink a beer on me. They served excellently they followed orders and they done their jobs with excellence and exerted and applied the authority that they were authorized to use, you should be very proud of those three men, their three of the finest troopers that I've ever had the privilege of traveling with, and

I thought they deserved to be able to sit down and enjoy two or three beers before reporting back in. If you have any problems with that general it's my fault, not theirs. They were only following my orders."

"I just wanted to make sure they wasn't dead, or that they had met some pretty women and decided not to come back, hell as far as I'm concerned, as long as they show up by tomorrow morning, everything's okay." Then the general stuck out his hand and added, "it's good to have you back Hightower, is the Carter problem over with?"

"I'll tell you the same thing I told everyone else general, I seen her go into the house and watched it burn to the ground. Did I see her die? No, I didn't. So I cannot swear that Elizabeth Carter is dead, but I am expecting word from the Sheriff of Las Cruces, New Mexico. After they go through the rubble, he is supposed to send me a report on how many bodies they find, and especially if they find Elizabeth Carter's body. So as it stands general you know as much right now, as I do. The only thing I can really tell you is that I am so damn glad to be home. Now I have a question to asked you Sir, just how bad have you and my wife spoiled my dogs, I know that everyone in this stockade and in that ranch house has spoiled those two children."

"I don't know if the dogs have been spoiled or not Edward, but I do know that they have been trained extensively by Rachel and you father-in-law. I think even Dorothy has gotten into the act. I do know for a fact that they are very protective of those babies. Your wife and her sister gives those dogs a bath every Saturday, and brushes their hair our and when they're finished those two dogs, they shine like new money." The general scratched his head and looked at Edward in a very questioning way and ask, "do you want me to have a squad of men move their tents, half of them in front, and half of them in the back of your house? , It won't be any trouble at all, because I'm having a problem of finding something for them to do. Because the Indians on the reservation are extremely peaceful and the people around here have found that out. They have even established that every Saturday afternoon and evening is set aside for a meal and just sharing time together while they learn each other's traditions. Some are even learning to speak their language and there is two school teachers that come out and teach the Indian children every Saturday morning and Sunday afternoon after church, all in all, it's been real peaceful.

As Hightower stood talking to the general, the general pointed behind him and said, here comes your wife. The judge was driving the buck board and he was in no hurry, the judge had a thing about going fast, he didn't like it. Judge Tatum would say, "life goes by fast enough, why push it any faster." Turning back to face the general Hightower said, "if you're a mind to general, I think the ladies would enjoy you showing up for supper tonight. That is, unless you got something else you need to do, and if so, I'm quite sure that you can have a rain check. I'm not joking when I say that I am looking forward to having a good home-cooked meal and I don't care what it is, I know it's going to taste good.!

Opening the gate to the pasture and heading the big gray into the field, Hightower took off his bridle and instantly the big gray started running and bucking and then he fell down on the ground and started rolling in the dust. It was as if he had been turned loose after being cooped up for two or three years, Instead of two or three months. He closed the gate and hung the bridal on the gate post, and then he just stood there watching the big gray for a few minutes and then under his breath he said, "enjoy yourself big boy, you've earned it."

Then Hightower turned and started walking toward the house and for some reason or another, even though he had gotten a good night sleep on the train, he felt as if he could lay down and take a nap. Maybe it was simply because the tension was gone, and he could relax at least for a little while. When he walked into the house, he didn't see the babies so we asked Rachel, "what have you done with the kids,? I'd sure like to able to spend some time with them."

"Oh, you'll get to spend plenty of time with them, but if I was you I wouldn't try to go in the bedroom just yet, Rachel said with a smile on her face. "Why Hightower ask?" That's when Dorothy spoke up and said, "those two puppies, and I am quite sure, "Mr. Hightower," that if you tried to get close to those two babies without first getting acquainted with those dogs, you would have quite a fight on your hands." Hightower seemingly disappointed said, "if I can't see my kids, or pet my dogs, can I at least have a big glass of Sweet tea?" Rachel spoke up with a very soft vice and taunting smile on her face and said, "why, Mr. Hightower, you can have anything you want." Dorothy spoke up and said in between giggles, "Edward Hightower, I honestly believe that your are blushing."

Changing the subject very quickly. Hightower said without looking at either Rachel or Dorothy, "I suppose that you have already named both of the dogs, so I would really like to know which one is which and what their names are?"

"Before you left. Edwards you came up with two sets of names, one was King and Queenie, the other was Bo and Josie. So all we did was take one name from one set and the other name from the other set. SO the dogs names are, King for the boy dog, and Josie for the girl dog. They have been trained to answer to their names and to respond by coming to you and setting down. But they will only do what when you are holding one of the babies. You can call their names right now, and they will stop and look at you, but they will not come to a stranger and let's face it Edward to them you are a stranger. So might I suggest that you make it a point to take me for a walk every day until they get used to you, and know that you are their master," "Rachel, I have never been someone's master, not even with Comanche, we are partners and that is the way I want these dogs to feel. If you would go into the room and get me the little girl so that I can hold her for a little while. I believe if Josie sees me holding the baby that she will realize I am no threat to the baby or her."

Before Rachel could move Dorothy said, "sit still sis, I'll go and get Rebecca." Hightower leaned back in his chair and ask, "by the way, who came up with the name Rebecca Marie?"

This time it was just the judge's voice that Hightower heard, "Edward, Rebecca Marie was the name of my wife's baby sister who died when she was still young of rheumatic fever. But it was Rachel, who suggested the name, I guess we should have mentioned it to you in a telegram, but we all figured you had enough on your mind without reminding you that you were a father of a beautiful set of twins, one boy, one girl. Rachel felt if we told you that the babies had been born that it would distract you and it may even cause you to take chances that you normally wouldn't take just so you could get back and hold them. With a woman like Elizabeth Carter and the men who rode with her one moments distraction could be enough to get you killed. So Edward, if you want to blame somebody for the children's names I guess you can blame us all, We talked about it for a long while and decided that it would be the best thing to do."

"Ain't nobody mad judge, I appreciate the reason for not telling me that the twins had been born. And I am not the least bit upset about what they were named. I never expected the boy to be named after me, and I had no idea about the girl, so everyone done me a favor, and to tell you the truth judge, I kinda like the name Rebecca Marie. I can just picture Rachel sticking her head out the back door hollering, "Becky you better get your little fanny back up here."

The judge put his elbows on the table and said, "sounds like Amy when she was trying to get Rachel's attention." Amy spoke up and said, "you were just as bad, admit it."

Dorothy appeared from the hallway with Rebecca cradled in her arms and Josie right behind her, when she handed the baby to Hightower Josie sat down on the floor at his feet, facing him. Hightower took Rebecca in his hands, and leaned forward and showed the baby to Josie so that she could satisfy her curiosity that the baby was in no danger. Then, Hightower slowly crossed his legs making a cradle for the baby and placed the baby onto his lap, and called Josie's name and she immediately put her front feet on Hightower's leg and looked down at the baby and sniffed her, then looked at Hightower and very gently removed her feet from his legs and curled up on the floor right at his feet. Putting his hand down close to Josie. He let her smell it, and then he patted her on the head very gently. All this time, the family had been quiet Rachel finally broke the silence by saying, "she remembers you Edward, but I think King might be a little harder to get close to."

"It'll just take time Rachel.", Hightower said. Then he just happened to remember about the general. So Hightower being apologetic said, "I hope y'all don't mind but I invited the general for supper."

Amy was the first one that spoke up saying, "it's a fine time to tell us, come on girls, let's get something on the stove." "Really, Rachel said, you could have notified us before now it's going to take at least two hours to prepare a decent meal, and it's already 5 o'clock." "Rachel, I really don't think the general is looking for some kind of a feast, I think that he would probably just enjoy the company of some very pretty ladies for a little while, instead of those long legged, harry faced troopers that he sees everyday." While Hightower was talking. He had one hand on the baby and the other hand, was petting Josie.

Dorothy came over the Hightower and picked up Rebecca and said, "it's time for you to meet your son Edward, I'll lay Rebecca down and bring Junior and King back in here. Be careful of King now, he is even more protective than Josie is." As Dorothy disappeared through the door going into the bedroom Josie was right on her heels with her ears perked up and her tail wagging and as Dorothy laid Rebecca down in her crib Josie stood on her hind legs and watched as Rebecca was laid down and covered with a blanket. Seeing that Rebecca was in no danger and was quite content Josie laid down in front for the crib and closed her eyes.

Hightower was still setting in the same position when Dorothy entered the room carrying Junior and true to form King was right behind her, watching every move she made. King stopped suddenly and perked up his ears then walked over to Hightower and placed his front feet on Hightower's leg and smelled his hand, then his tail started wagging and it was plain to see that King remembered him, so with a nudge with his nose, Hightower started petting him on the head and talking to him and King responded with a whine and then he laid down next to Hightower and acted as if he was going to go to sleep.

Amy spoke up saying, "I've always been told that animals are good judges of characters, so it seems that King has voiced his complete approval of you Edward, but I was quite certain that he would be a bit harder to get close to." Then she turned back to the girls and said, "let's get cooking."!

It was hard for Hightower to believe just how much his life had changes in the past year and a half. He had went from a lowly Army scout to being married, owning his own ranch, becoming a father twice over and wearing a badge that gave him authority that he never believed possible. The most unbelievable thing that had happened was when general Whitehead decided to build his outpost right on the edge of the small reservation and with in a quarter of a mile of his house. Not many people can say that his family is protected by the US cavalry when he has to go on the road.

He also couldn't believe how fast those two border Collie puppies had grown, and just how well Rachel, Dorothy, and Amy had trained them to protect the two most precious things in his life, his son, and his daughter.

Although he was quite sure that those border Collie's would be more than glad to protect everyone in that house, especially the three women.

They had been sitting around the kitchen table, talking back and forth while the women fixed supper, and no one had noticed what time it was suddenly they were aware of someone knocking on the front door. The judge said, "I need to stretch my legs anyway, I'll get it." With that he started for the front door, but when he opened the front door. There was no one there, just a telegram addressed to Edward Hightower, senior.

The judge brought the telegram back into the kitchen and handed it to Edward. Dorothy said, "here let me take Junior, and I'll put him back in his crib until he's ready to be fed and you can read your telegraph."

Opening up the envelope Hightower began to read and the longer he read the bigger the smile was on his face. The telegram had came from three other lawmen. The three signatures were, Wade Jackson, Dan Willows, and Matthew Rivers. The message was short and straight to the point. "Congratulations on becoming a father, stop. Will see you soon have new from Las Cruces". Hightower handed the telegraph to the judge and then he handed it to Rachel. "Are those three outlaws coming to this house?, Rachel ask with a smile on her face." "I don't know Rachel, I don't think they'll all three show up at the same time, because that would leave pretty much half of the state of Texas, without the presence of the most outstanding law men in the state. It doesn't say when they're going to show up so we'll all have to stick pretty close to the house and I guess we'll all have to get together and make room for them, because there is no way that I'm going to allow them to stay in a hotel that far away from the ranch. I have ridden or worked with every one of these men, and I'm here to tell you right now. There is not three other men in this world that I would rather ride with. They are fair, and they will even give the worst criminal a chance. I don't know of very many outlaws that would consider standing in the middle of the Street. Even if they had 10 men backing them up, and face these three lawmen I'll swear that all three of these men are so fast they can draw and fire and you will never see it."

The judge spoke up and said, "there's one more that needs to be added to that list, and that's you. Edward. You've forgot that I have seen you use the Hog leg, and I have noticed that you just don't miss, you hit exactly what you're aiming at."

Just about that time, there came a knock on the back, the judge jumped up and said, "maybe this is another telegram." Going to the back door he opened it and found the general standing on the back porch in full uniform, evidently he had taken himself a bath and shaved and slicked his hair back and had his orderly press him out a uniform and shine his boots, and because the general was truly spit and polished from head to toe. In his hand he carried three bouquets of flowers, "with your permission, Mr. Hightower," he handed Rachel a bouquet of flowers also. Each of the ladies thanked him very lady like and each one in turn kissed him on the cheek.

The judge jumped up and said, "I don't know about you gentlemen, but a good stiff shot of whiskey has always helped my appetite. How about it? Would you gentlemen care to join me, and partake of let's say about three fingers."

"Why don't you gentlemen go on in to the living room and set down for a while and drink your whiskey, it's still going to be at least another 30 minutes before supper is ready and I for one would thank you to get out from under my feet.", Amy said, this with her hands on her hips and a little bit of flour on her left cheek and a wink at the judge, just to let him know that she wasn't serious.!

Hightower and the general followed the judge into the living room and he poured about three fingers of whiskey into the three glasses and handed each glass to its owner and said, "here's to the whole cockeyed bunch being together anytime soon. Here's to keeping your fingers crossed."

The general raised his glass and clicked Edwards and then the judges glass. Then after taking a sip of the whiskey. He looked at Hightower and ask, "I do hope there wasn't anything bad in that telegram. I tried to get the telegraph operator to tell me what was in it, but he said it was against the law for anybody to read that telegram until you did. Can you believe that Cpl. would not let me read that telegram. I'm kind of proud of that young man, he showed some backbone, I just might give him another stripe. "Then the general laughed and asked the judge, "do you think a fellow might get a refill judge?" The judge was up and out of his chair in a flash, and all he said was, "damn general, I thought you would never ask."

Hightower looked at the general and said, "general, when these three men get here, I guarantee you that this will be the safest place in the state of Texas. There's going to be three US marshals and one Texas Ranger and a whole troop of cavalry within a quarter of a mile circle around this ranch house. Now if that's not protection, I don't know what is.!"

The judge spoke up and said, "general, why can we put our a big barbecue for every body the day they get here?." "Sounds good to me, they probably could stand a break," the general said as the judge filled his glass again.

It wasn't very long at all until Dorothy appeared and said, "if you would care to join us gentlemen supper is ready." Then she disappeared back into the dining room. When everyone was seated, the judge tapped his glass with a fork and said, "we're going to do something tonight that we have gotten away from. And I think it's time we started it back, Mama, would you please say grace?"

"If everyone will please join hands and bow your heads, Amy said." Then with a quiver in her voice. She began, "Lord, we thank you for this food and we pray for that safety of everyone in this house and we thank you for the return of our beloved Edward. We thank you for the two puppies that you have granted us and now we pray that Dorothy will soon decide to say yes to a young man that is about to propose marriage, amen."

No sooner had Amy said, amen than Dorothy said, "Mama, I'm not ready for marriage yet. I'm only 17 and I would like to be courted by more than one man, you make it sound like I'm going to be an old maid before I turn 19."

"Now Dorothy, everyone at this table knows that you have a soft spot in your heart for young Mr. Mason, and everyone at this table knows that he is head over heels in love with you, but if you are not the least bit interested in him then I will forbid him to keep meeting you on the back porch every evening after dark," the judge said while staring down at his plate.

"I didn't say I didn't want to see him anymore, or that I would not at least consider marriage to him, but the general knows very well that we can't get married as long as he is in the Army, simple because there is no living quarters for married troopers."

"Trooper Mason has the makings of becoming a very distinguished soldier and if someone of rank was to nominated him for officers candidate school. Then there could be quarters established for married officers, but that could only be done if trooper Mason wanted to make a career out of the US cavalry. There would be no sense in promoting him to second Lieut. if he was going to leave the Army in the next year when his enlistment is up. If you would like me to, miss Dorothy, I will find out what trooper Mason has on his mind about reenlisting and if he would be interested in going to officers candidate school or if he intends to leave the Army and return to the civilian side of life." The general said.

Hightower spoke up and said, "I've got a remedy in mind. If anyone should care to hear my point of view." Dorothy spoke up saying, "go ahead Edward, speak your piece." Hightower spoke very quickly and in plain language saying, "I fully intend to add on to this house because this family has never been separated and I can see no reason why it should be separated now. With me not knowing when I have to leave or when I do leave how long I'll be gone. It would be a great relief to me to know that Rachel is not in this house by herself. I propose right now that the judge and Ms. Amy considers this their home and Dorothy, I want you and Mr. Mason to feel the same way it would be of great relief to me to know that when I am gone, there will be a man here to take care of the ranch and all the contents thereof. Why don't you discuss that with Mr. Mason Dorothy. Personally I count the young man as a friend and I think he would make you a very good husband."!

Of course we can sit here and talk about this all night, but it doesn't mean a thing until we talk to Mason and see what his intentions are. He may very well want to stay in the Army and take a shot at officers candidate school. If he doesn't want to stay in the Army and he doesn't want to live in this house I'm quite sure that we could build another house two or one hundred feet from this one just for Dorothy and Mason, but like Edward said, we don't know which way to go until we talk to Mr. Mason." Amy said while she was cleaning the table off of the flowers that was in the middle of the table so that she could start placing the food to where it could be passed.

Hightower looked at Rachel and said, "if the babies are on solid food, I would sure love to feed on of them." "I'm afraid Mr. Hightower that you cannot feed the children yet, simply because they are not on solid food strictly on a liquid diet." Once again, Hightower's cheeks became flushed simply because he knew that everyone in the room knew Rachel was still breast-feeding. The redder Hightower's cheeks got the more Dorothy and

Rachel giggled until they finally couldn't hold it in any longer, the judge, Gen. Whitehead, and Amy just burst out laughing the only thing Hightower could do was join in, so he did.

The women had outdone themselves with this meal, there was a large platter full of steaks, a large bowl of mashed potatoes, there was green beans, corn, biscuits and gravy, and on the stove was a large peach cobbler still hot and bubbling.

The general looked over at Miss Amy and said with a great big smile, "are you sure that you wouldn't consider joining our troop and relieving Mr. Dean?." "No Sirree Bob, Amy said, I've got enough of an army right here."

As the food was passed around and everyone fill there plates, conversation went from subject to subject. Hightower brought up the subject that he wanted to raise a few cows, and Rachel wants a chicken coop built in such a way as to keep the chicken hawks and the weasel out simply because they were eating a dozen eggs every morning for breakfast and it didn't count the eggs that were used in making cornbread or others dishes. She said they needed to have between 30 and 40 hens laying at a time, just to keep up with the use of all the eggs needed.

Gen. Whitehead told Rachel that the Army would buy all of the eggs that she wanted to sell and if she agreed to that, he would have the men build her a nice chicken house and it would house as many chicken as she wanted and he would designate certain men to take care of the feeding of the chickens in the morning and in the afternoon, all she would have to do was collect the eggs.

Rachel was one of these people that never jumped into anything, so she told the general that she needed some time to think it over, cause she couldn't let the raising of the chickens interfere with the time that she spent with the twins. That's when Dorothy spoke up and said, "don't forget Rachel, I haven't left home yet, I can help with the chickens in any way and at any time, so don't you worry about taking time away from the babies, that won't happen." The general spoke up and said, "I'll have the men start on the chicken house first thing in the morning if that's all right with you, Rachel?" She just nodded her head yes.

Chapter 2

Having finished their meal all three men, after thanking the women for a delicious meal retired to the front porch, but along the way they stopped and got another three fingers of whiskey. When they settled down on the front porch as far as Hightower was concerned the conversation turned ugly. The general simply asked one question and the whole evening took a different tone.

"Edward, what happens if they can't find Elizabeth Carter's body?" Hightower scratched his head, then took a long pull on the glass of whiskey, then he very solemnly said, "I guess I'll try to pick up her trail and the next time I'll have to execute the second half of that warrant.

The judge spoke up and asked, "what's on your mind Edward,? You don't seem to be yourself. Every time the subject of Elizabeth Carter comes up, you seem to withdraw. Are you worried about what people will think of a man who brings a woman and to be hanged?, If that's what's bothering you, I suggest you look at it this way, the woman to date has been personally responsible for the death of her last husband, one of her stepsons, not to mention the two deputies that were taking her to prison, that was murder in cold blood. The attempt on Rachel's life that she ordered, now we get to all the bank robberies that her and her gang performed. At last but not least the ordering of the murder of the biggest Sheriff of Las Cruces New Mexico. There is no reason in this world why you should feel any guilt about ending the life of a woman who has caused so much pain and misery, not only to the families of the lawmen she had killed, but the families of the civilians that were murdered in cold blood, just so people would know her name. It's your duty Edward, not only because you are the only one that can identify her, but you have to bring her in for the sake of your family, because that crazy unfeeling woman I fear will try to hurt you and your family again."

"I know what's at stake judge, you don't have to tell me. If she is still alive, it won't be as easy as people thanks to bring her in. She is most certainly crazy, but I don't think anyone should ever think that Elizabeth Carter is stupid. because she's not. She's very cunning and the best things that I can remember about her, she pays an awful good game of chess. She knows how to plan, if I'm catch her, I need to play a damn good game of chess myself. Every move that she'll make will be planned exactly like a game of chess, four or five moves ahead and she will not go down until she has used every ounce of strength that she has. I will not make mistake of presuming that she is dead again, but we're getting ahead of ourselves. This could be all for nothing, she very likely did die when the house was burnt. One way or the other, I'll know when Wade Jackson gets here." After taking another drink of his whiskey, Hightower repeated, "one way or the other"!!!

The general finished his drink of whiskey and said, "if you gentlemen will please pardon me for my swift departure, I just seen Andrews, Lewis, and Mason, go into the chow hall, and I want to have a few words with them. To answer your question before you ask it Edward, no they're not in trouble. There is only one question I would like to ask you, if you have to go after her again, would you want to use these three men again?"

Hightower leaned back in his chair and looked directly at the general and without blinking an eye said, "yes Sir, but I don't want you to order them to ride with me, I want them to volunteer, after all, this is my fight, not theirs."

"As you wish," the general said as he rose from his chair and started off of the porch. "I will see you gentlemen sometime tomorrow morning when you show the men where you want this chicken house built, until then, thanks for the meal and thank the ladies for me for the very enjoyable company, good night."

Hightower and the judge sat there watching the general walk in the directions of the mess Hall, and the judge commented, "there goes a man with a lot on his shoulders, but he carries it well. I don't know about you Edward, but I'm going to get me another three fingers of whiskey, this conversation has just slightly upset my stomach." Continuing to set in his chair with his feet propped up on the railing, the thought came to Hightower's mind, "what if, what if," there was just too many questions that Hightower didn't have the answer to. For his own sake, he had to end this. He had to remove any threat there was to Rachel and the twins, and he had to do it as quickly as he possibly could, but there was nothing he could do until he had talked to Wade Jackson.

He had settled deep in thought, when the three ladies and the judge rejoined him on the porch. Each lady carried with her a cup of coffee, Rachel had two, one of her, and one of him. It was as if she could read his mind!.

For the rest of the evening nothing was said about Elizabeth Carter, the conversation went from the chicken house, to the dogs and how they were around the babies, and of course there was a lengthy conversation about Junior and Rebecca and the cute things they would do, the way that both of them laughed, the way they played with their feet, and when they were laid on a blanket in the floor how they would pull and tug at King and Josie and how the dogs seem to enjoy it when the babies touch them.

As they set on the porch enjoying family time Rachel noticed that troopers was carrying their gear into their bunkhouse and she remarked, "from the looks of what's going on down there, the general has placed a guard around the house again. Those 10 men will stand two hour shifts around the house front and back, just the same as before you left. Edward." Then she leaned forward and whispered in Edward's ear, "if you have to go after her again Edward, end her, don't let her cause any more turmoil in this family." Then she kissed him in the cheek and excused herself by saying, "it's been quite a rambunctious day for me, so I'm going to turn in." Then with a smile and a wink at Hightower, she turned and walked back into the house.

Hightower turned his head toward the front door and said, "I need to go check on Comanche, and then I'm going to turn in too." He said it loud enough so he was sure that Rachel heard him. He was just about to go off of the porch. When he heard Amy tell the judge, "looks like tomorrow's going to be a big day. So I suggest we turn in too."

As he walked toward the corral, Hightower thought to himself that he mustn't let Elizabeth Carter, if she is alive, to manipulate his life anymore. As much as he didn't want to be known as a lawman who shot a woman, if it came right down to it, and there was no other way, he would take her down.! Even as rowdy as Bell Star was she was still a woman and deserved to be treated like one. He hadn't known Bell Star personally, but he had spoken to a lot of people who did and it was said that she could be as much of a lady as anyone from the East and well bred. Why she picked the life she did, only she knew and it died with her.

Comanche seemed to know that something was on Hightower's mind, because when he seen Hightower walking toward the corral he perked up his ears and galloped over the fence and stuck its head over and nuzzled Hightower as he climbed up on the fence to rub the big gray stallion's neck and stroke his ears and spend just a few minutes talking to him. Hightower had spent quite a few evenings alone at a campsite, with no one to talk but Comanche, so he could Comanche things that he couldn't tell people. He could explain his feelings to Comanche without fear of it ever going any further. The big gray could sense when Hightower was tense or exceptionally alert, and like a good partner he would develop the same actions and alertness. It was almost as if the horse could read Hightower's mind. After a few minutes of rubbing the big gray's forehead, ears, and his neck, Hightower decided it was time to turn in. As it had became a custom with Rachel and Hightower, they always talked for a little while before they went to sleep. They could discuss things in the privacy of their bedroom away from prying eyes and listening ears. Because of the babies. Their bedroom was on the first floor of the house. All of the other bedroom were upstairs and at the rear of the house. Hightower had spent many a night, just setting on the balcony at the back of the house, just listening to the owls whippoorwill's and every once in a while the howl of a coyote. These sounds would make him yearn for the quietness in the solitude of the Texas Badlands. But right now he was longing to spend some very special time with Rachel, alone with no interruptions. There was a time in Hightower's life when he presumed that he would spend the rest of his life alone, but Rachel had changed his mind about that, he wanted to spent the rest of his life, sharing everything with her and being there watching the twins grow up.

Elizabeth Carter was not going to interfere with his life, or threaten his family and extended family every again. This was a promise that he made to himself, and he didn't make a habit of breaking promises.

Before he entered the bedroom he took his boots off in the hallway so that the sound of the heals of his boots would not wake the twins up. He moved very slowly and as quietly as possible. He hanged his shirt and jeans across the back of the chair and he crawled into bed. As he lay there in the bed on his back, he thought back to the time when he made the trip to Lake Charles that brought him in contact with judge Tatum and eventually Rachel and he wondered at just how much his life had changed in the course of a couple of years, then staring at the ceiling he said very quietly, "thank you Lord, not only for saving my life, but for protecting my wife and children and my wife's family, bless them, please and keep them sake ALWAYS."

Then he turned over on his side and as he got comfortable Rachel cuddled up to his back and put her arm around him, pulling herself closer. The next thing that he knew was seeing Rachel seated in the chair with a baby in each arm and a smile on her face as she nursed both babies at the same time. she would never realize just how proud he was of her, and how she made up for every bad thing he had ever seen. She would never know just how peaceful he felt inside whenever he was around her. He finally knew what being in love felt like and that feeling was something he never wanted to lose.!

It had started to rain sometime during the night and the sound of the rain striking the window pane and the gentle roll of thunder and the occasional lightning bolt that would light up the night seemed to have a calming affect and made it easier to sleep.

Rachel had turned the lamp down really low and had slid back into bed and as she cuddled up next to him and lay her head on the pillow. She whispered, "I loved the life we have, and I never want anything to change, good night my love." Then she was asleep and as he gazed at her face he could see the contentment, and it made him feel even more at ease.

When he awoke the next morning Rachel had already bathed the babies, change the diapers, and fed them. He could hear the babies as they lay on a blanket on the floor in the dining room playing with King and Josie. While Rachel, along with Amy and Dorothy were fixing breakfast. Why she hadn't woke him up he didn't know. He could hear the judge talking to the girls as they fixed breakfast, so he got up and reached for his shirt and jeans, where he had laid them the night before, but he found a freshly ironed shirt and a pair of clean jeans and socks. Everything that he had in his jeans pockets was laid on the small nightstand beside the bed and his boots were setting on the floor next to the bed. After he had dressed he turned up the light, so he could see in the mirror to comb his hair. Then after deciding that there wasn't much that he could do to make himself any prettier he turned out the lamp and healed for the kitchen.

As he walked into the kitchen, he heard the judge say, "Howdy stranger, I was beginning to think you were going to sleep all day." Then with a laugh. He continued, "I reckon it feels might good to be back home, I know it feels awful good to the rest of us to have you back."

"Would you believe that is the first honest to goodness night sleep that I have had in over three months. I slept as sound as a baby and I really don't think I moved all night, where's the coffee cups?" He was quickly told by his wife to, "set down and I'll get you a cup, I don't know if you moved during the night or not, because I slept sounders last night than I have in all the time that you were gone."

"What time did it start rain in last night judge? Hightower ask." "I don't know. Edward, but it sound like it has setting in for a good while. I know it hasn't eased up since I was awakened by a loud crash of thunder a little after 5 o'clock this morning."

"Has anyone made a pot of coffee for the troopers that are on the back porch, and the front porch. At least they're not having to stand there post in the rain?" Dorothy spoke up and said, "yes father, I took care of that the very first thing this morning, and each man was also given two large sausage biscuit, I hope that was all right?" "Of course it was, Amy said."

Hightower took a sip of the cup of coffee that Rachel had placed before him and then he said, "if it ever stops raining. I need to take a trip around the place and see what need to be fixed. The last thing we need is cattle all over the countryside or horses out running wild. I reckon it's time that I started thinking about hiring at least a couple of hands to live and work on this ranch."

Being that it was still raining, after Hightower had finished his breakfast. He preceded to get down on the floor with the babies and play with them, just to show King and Josie that the babies were safe when he was around. He also spent some time with both dogs petting them, and talking to them at one time he even got a game of tug-of-war going with Josie. And then he started a game of fetch with King and Josie joined in, and it wasn't long before the living room and dining room had the appearance of a room filled with children playing tag. The babies were laughing and the dogs were barking and finally, Rachel came in and sat down on the floor saying, "it sounds to me like you're having as much fun as the babies and the dogs put together."

"I reckon I am Rachel, I haven't felt this much at ease in a long time, life is definitely good, and I look for it to get even better." The laughter and the playing continued until Rachel finally said, "I'm sorry, Edward, but it's time for these two young roustabout's to take a nap. Would you mind letting King and Josie out for just a little while, they've been in the house all night and really need to go outside."

Hightower answered her by saying, "let me get another cup of coffee and I'll walk out on the porch and set for a while till they come back from doing their morning running." "You'll probably be out there for a little while because the dogs have a couple of friends over at the stockade that they visit every morning and then they come by the mess Hall, Mr. Dean always has some kind of treat to give them, most generally he keeps back a couple of T-bones instead of throwing the bones in the garbage. He picks out two real nice ones, and saves them for the next morning. Mr. Dean sets and talks to the dogs while they chew on their bones, he seems to really enjoy their company. Even a few of the troopers will play fetch with the dogs. The general doesn't mind. He says it gives the men the chance to exercise right along with the dogs."

Before going onto the porch Hightower helped Rachel with the two babies. Then when they were in their cribs and tucked in Hightower turned and said to the dogs, "does anyone want to go outside?" Both dogs started spinning in circles and Hightower looked at Rachel with a questioning look on his face and Rachel smiled and said, "that's their way of telling you to open the door they need to go, and I suggest that you start moving, Mr. Hightower, or it's going to be " You" cleaning up a mess!"

Without hesitating Hightower made a beeline for the front door and the dogs were out the door at a dead run, and it seemed that they didn't care if it was raining or not, they didn't touch a step going off of the porch they just jumped and headed in the direction of the trees down by the creek. Easing down into a chair with his coffee Hightower watched the two dogs as hey disappeared into the trees that line the Creek bank. The rain was still coming down at a pretty good clip and there was a chill from all of the moisture in the air, there was a blanket that Rachel used to put acrossed her shoulders when she sat on the porch when it rained, so he reached over and got the blanket and put it crossed his shoulders and then he realized why she would do that. The blanket kept the back of his neck and his shoulders quite warm. And believe it or not, the longer he set there with that blanket on his shoulders, the sleepier he got. So, not wanting to look like someone 60 years old, he took the blanket off and laid it down across his lap" he was still sitting drinking his coffee when Rachel came out the door carrying a coffee pot, and without saying a word, she filled his cup, kissed him on the cheek, and went back inside.

The rain seem to be picking up so Hightower decided he would just spent the day lounging around. It was king of nice to sit on your own front porch with your feet propped up and a good hot cup of coffee and no pressure. There was nothing pushing him, and there was nothing he had to chase, all he had to do was set back and enjoy life and being with his family, without the threat of an unwanted interruption.

It had been about an hour and a half since King and Josie had bolted off of the front porch. Those two young dogs lived and breathed. Herding animals like cattle, goats, sheep, hell they would even try to herd chickens, until a rooster got tired of begin pushed and then they knew when to head for the house. It was kind of funny watching the rooster, the dogs would go into different directions, and there was only one rooster and he couldn't decide which one he wanted to chase. He would run three or four steps after King, then he would turn around and chase Josie for about the same distance, then he would quit and just scratched the ground with the feathers on his neck all ruffled up and his wings outstretched. I guess he was just showing everyone that he was not the happiest bird in the yard, but it was funny anyway.!!

The judge came out and sat down with his cup of coffee and within a couple of minutes here come Amy and Dorothy carrying a large rocking crib, and right behind them was Rachel with the babies, one in each arm. Each one was wearing pajamas that Amy Rachel and Dorothy had me. What it consisted of looked like a long night shirt that come down six or 8 inches below their feet, which didn't matter a whole lot because both babies had booties on. They were laid in the crib their heads at opposite ends of the crib and a light blanket was laid over both babies. Then all three ladies pulled up a chair and sat down.

Amy looked over at Hightower and said, "just listen to that rain, it's going to be so good for the garden, and for the pasture. There shouldn't be any shortage of hay or straw next winter." Hightower stretched his arms our and then turned his hands, palm up and ask," have you ladies put any thought into what kind of a schedule or what ever you want to call it that you're going to work out concerning this chicken house. One person cannot do it all. Even with two troopers feeding the chickens the Coop still need to be cleaned out, freshwater needs to put in watering troughs and then the eggs have to be gathered morning and night. Then one of you must keep track of how many eggs the cavalry uses. I tell you right now that raising these chicken is going to be more of a job than you think. You have to inspect that chicken house every morning to make sure that no weasels or any other kind of animal has burrowed into the chicken house. I really think you should ask general Whitehead about putting a wood floor in so that nothing can tunnel into the chicken house." "Don't get your pigtails in a knot, Mr. Hightower. We three have already mentioned that to the general and he agreed that we should do that, and he insisted that we need to use this newfangled window screen to keep snakes out or any other small rodent that would endanger the chickens. You take care of catching outlaws and killers, and we'll take care of the chickens. "Rachel said with her hands on her hips and her feet planted squarely on the porch. There are things on this ranch that I want to be my responsibility. I need to take the responsibility of something besides raising those two children. You put your life on the life every time you leave here to make sure that other people are safe, you never leave here without making sure that we are all safe all of us, Mama, Poppa, Dorothy, all of us, so please Edward, don't deny me the privilege of pulling my fair share."

"Rachel, I never in my life since I've known you, denied you anything, and I never will. If you want to raise them chickens and sell them eggs, then sweetheart you do what's going to make you feel good, but remember this, you are not my slave. I will not ask you to do anything that I won't do myself. I know how you must feel, you want to do something that you feel can make a difference in not only our way of life, but in other people's way of life. Now, maybe you will understand why I wear this badge, I want my life to stand for something, and when I'm gone. All I ask is that people say Edward Hightower was good, fair man."

Getting up out of his chair. Edward said, "excuse me folks, but I need to go down to the stockade and send a telegram." And without waiting for anyone to say anything, he stepped off of the porch and to Rachel. He looked funny walking down through the yard toward the general's office, without his gun belt on. He wasn't even carrying his Winchester and that worried her. At this very moment he had no way of protecting himself.

Amy looked over at Rachel and with a stern look on her face she said, "Rachel, I think you hit a nerve in your husband." "You didn't hit a nerve he's got a lot on his mind, and if he doesn't talk about it to somebody. It's going to eat at him, and eat at him, until his nerves get so raw that he will have to do something to ease that tension. Don't you know that he is worried that they won't find Elizabeth Carter's body in that rubble. That means he's going to have to go after her again and this time will have to be final time. He worries what people will think about a Marshall, who might possibly have to put a bullet in a woman. That, my dears is a hard thing for any man, especially a law man to have to live with." After saying this, the judge turned his head and went back in the house.

There was silence on the porch, the only sound was the rocking of the crib and from the inside of the house. The ladies could hear the judge, rattling some glass, which meant that he was pouring him a drink of whiskey. This told Amy that the judge was worried too, he didn't want to be the judge that sentenced a woman to hang, even if she was guilty of at least five murders and twice that many bank robberies.

Dorothy was the first one to speak, "I think it must be this rain that is causing everyone's nerves to wear thin. Everyone in this house is used to doing things outside, and being cooped up in this house is just a little bit unnerving. I mean the dishes are done, the best are made, the babies are fed and clothed, the only thing that hasn't been done is to get some towels and be ready to wipe King and Josie off. When they finally decided to come home. You know they're going to be soaking wet and we've got to dry them before we let them in the house. Even the troopers are not moving around outside, the only ones that are outside are the gentleman in the towers. Everyone else is either on the back porch, in the barn or helping Mr. Dean in the Chow Hall. So please before anyone else gets upsets and maybe says something that they shouldn't, let's all find something to do. Mama, if you don't mind, would you allow Rachel and I to help you with that new quit that you're making?"

"That's a good idea Dorothy, what do you think Rachel? Are you up to maybe sticking a needle in your finger?" Amy said with a smile on her face "I think maybe sticking a needle in my finger might be the very think to remind me to keep my big mouth shut, and not to speak harshly to one of the few really good men in Texas. That woman Elizabeth Carter is till causing problems in this family and I know just how much Edward wants her to go away. And I understand that around here, people could identify Elizabeth Carter, but away from Lake Charles, there's no one to identify her, except Edward. He's going to have to find her or our lives will be spent walking around on pins and needles just hoping that someone doesn't say something that brings it to ahead. I know it's not the Christian thing to say, Mama, but Elizabeth Carter need to rot in hell for the things that she has done and the people that she has hurt."

With that Rachel and Dorothy picked up the cradle while Amy held the door open, they carried the babies back inside into the living room where Amy had been working on her quilt. Dorothy spoke up and said, "I'm going to get me a cup of coffee, does anyone else want one?" "If you girls won't tell your father, I feel like pouring me three fingers of whiskey." "Go ahead Mama," came a voice from the kitchen, "it might help you to stop being such a sour old woman," Then a smile came across Amy's face as she heard her husband laugh at least three times. The girls also thought it was funny and just like that. The tension was gone, and there was peace and love once again on the rocking H ranch.

In the meantime, while the women got settled down in the living room. Hightower walked slowly across the compound toward the general's office, but was diverted by Mr. Dean calling to him from the Chow Hall, so Hightower walked over to the Chow Hall, and Mr. Dean invited him inside and told him to sit down.

He then started a conversation by saying, "there's a chill in the air this morning that you don't normally find this time of year and as a little token of my appreciation for you making it back from that trip that you was on, I thought maybe a good hot cup of hot chocolate just might warm up those worry old bones of yours."

Hightower being just a little over 30 years old got a kick out of Mr. Dean treating him as if he were 60. Actually Mr. Dean was older than Hightower and it seemed quite a bit smarter. He had sensed there was a tension in Hightower that needed to be released and as Hightower's father once told him nothing can erase tension like a good hearty laugh and a little humor never hurt anyone.. It seemed that the years that he had spent with his father before he enlisted in the cavalry was finally sinking in and he was becoming more like his father every day. Then with a smile. Hightower spoke, "Mr. Dean, I thought you were only the cook around here, but it also seems that you are the camp philosopher. As a matter of fact, Sir, I would really enjoy that cup of hot chocolate."

The longer that Hightower and Mr. Dean talked, the lighter the load on Hightower shoulders became and he soon found himself taking turns telling stories of the funny things that had happened to him in the first 10 years of his enlistment in the Army. He spoke of the humor that sometimes can be found in the middle of a conflict such as when his first commanding officer lost his balance in the middle of an attack and fell off his horse, the troopers thought the commander had been shot and everyone stopped and circled around him. When he had gotten his breath back, het sat up and said, and I quote, "who in the hell told you to stop?" Then he hollered at the top of his lungs, "charge" but while the men were surrounding the commanding officer the Indians had disappeared. There was one second Lieut., who knelt down beside the captain and ask very seriously, "which direction do we charge in Sir? The captain stood up and when he pointed in the direction of where the Indians used to be. He stopped in the middle of his order and said, "well Lieut., it looks like we don't charge at all, there's no Indians to charge at, where did they go?" Then one salty old stop Sgt. said, "I guess maybe Capt. the Indians thought this was not a serious charge with you. Just simply following off of your horse." The captain soon requested a transfer because he couldn't stand the men in his command knowing that he just simply fell off of his horse in the middle of a charge and lit flat on his ass. Before the captain was relieved and transferred he and that salty old top Sgt. went out and they both got drunk and had one of the damnedest fistfights that you ever seen, And the funniest. They were both so drunk that they would get no closer than 5 feet apart and would swing just as hard as they could and fall down, simply because they were in no condition to even stand, let alone fight. The men in the troop, the next morning, found both men still passed out lying face down on the ground with out so much as a bruise or a scratch on their body. So every member of the troops that was present made a vow that they would never allow that story to be told because of the embarrassment it brought to the entire troop.

By now, Mr. Dean had laughed so hard that he had tears in his eyes and between laughs he would say, "can you just imagine a captain sitting flat on his ass, in a cloud of dust, with his sword raised in the air, screaming at the top of his lungs, "charge,"!!! Then Mr. Dean would go into a another round of laughter. He finally laughed so hard that he feel off of his chair on to the hard floor, then with a surprised look on his face, He raised his right arm in the air and screamed, "charge". Hightower by this time had tears in his eyes and had given out a couple of real good belly laughs himself.

The general had heard the laughter going on in the Chow Hall, and had walked over and walked through the door and as he stood at the entrance. He caught Mr. Dean's eye, and Mr. Dean at a loss for words simply looked up at the general and raised his right arm and said, "charge". The general not understanding what had been going on, just stood there in amazement and Hightower turned and seen him, then motioned for him to come over and set down. Then to help the general understand Hightower told the whole story all over again, and by the time the story was finished, even the general had tears in his eyes.

General Whitehead turned to Mr. Dean and said in between laughs, "Sir, under no circumstances will you serve this beverage to the men in.

Chapter 3

Hightower spent the next couple of hours sitting in the living room talking to the judge and watching the women work on that quilt. Finally he told the judge, "I was started down to see the general when Mr. Dean distracted me, so I guess I had better get on down there and talk to the general. Besides, I need to send a telegram to Wade Jackson and find out just exactly when he's going to show up and if he's brining anyone with him."

"This time put your poncho on, it's still raining outside and I don't want you to come down with a cold, "Rachel said without looking up from the quilt. Getting his poncho and putting it on Hightower preceded to give Rachel a kiss and told her, "I'll be back in a while, in the meantime, I'll see if I can't find those two dogs and send them home, okay?"

For some reason right before he was to go out the front door. Hightower reached up on the wall and got his gun belt and strapped it on, and as always spun the cylinder in the 45 to make sure it was loaded. Replacing it in the holster. He glanced up and noticed that all three women and the judge were staring at him. He just shook his head while he was heading for the door and said, "from this day on I am not taking anything for granted, and neither should you."

When he opened the screen door, both of the dogs came into the living room and they were soaking wet. So Rachel and Dorothy each grabbed a towel and started rubbing them dry. It was plain to see that both dogs really enjoyed this. The last thing Hightower heard before he stepped off of the porch was Rachel telling King, "stand still you little dickens".

When he walked into the general's office, the general was setting behind the desk with a big cup of steaming coffee and a pile of papers in front of him. So Hightower said, "looks to me like you need to take a break general." Then he asked the general with a straight face, "did you enjoy your cup of hot chocolate Sir?"

The general looked over the top of his spectacles and said, "as a matter of fact I did, and if this rain doesn't stop I just might talk myself into having another cup. It sure seems to give you a warm feeling on the inside, and besides it taste good. What's on your mind Edward?" "I need to send a telegram to Wade Jackson, if it's all right with you?" "It's fine with me, but I don't really think you need to," reaching across his desk, he picked up and envelope and handed it to Hightower. The telegram, read simply, "be at your place day after tomorrow." Signed Wade Jackson."

"I wonder what's so damned important that Wade can't tell me in a telegram what's going on?" "I don't know the general said, but it's always been my experience that when a law man makes a special trip to see you, it's not good news, but then again. Knowing how you for law men feel about each other. He could just be pulling your chain." I don't think so general, Wade's sense of humor doesn't go very far. For him to send a telegram like that means that he has something upsetting to tell me, and I'll be you five dollars to a hole in a dough nut that I know what it's all about. It has to be about Elizabeth Carter. Maybe the Sheriff of Las Cruces found her body in the ashes, as least I hope so. I'm tired of chasing that bitch. I really shouldn't talk about her that way, but it's the way I feel general."

"It's the first time since you got back that I have seen you with your gun belt on, is there something I need to know? If there is now's the time to tell me." "It's nothing that I can put my finger on general, I just have a gut feeling and my gut has always been pretty reliable. I just decided it was time that I start taking things seriously, if she's not dead, she'll be coming. She fully intends to make me pay for bringing her son Raymond in to hang. She has the same outlook on life that Raymond did, Raymond thought that no one could hold him responsible for anything. He felt he was above the law and that nobody had the right to tell him anything, that was what his mama taught him, after all, why shouldn't she, that's the way she believes."

As Hightower and the general set talking, the door to his office opened and three troopers walked in. It was Andrews, Lewis, and Mason, and they immediately came to attention and Lewis ask permission to speak. The general just waved his hand and said, "go ahead" so Anderson spoke up, "Hightower, if that woman is not dead, and she has formed another gang, the three of us are volunteering our services to help remedy this problem once and for all. We just wanted to let you know what if you need us we're ready and willing."

"I appreciate you three, but right now I won't know anything for sure until Wade Jackson gets here day after tomorrow, so just hang back and be ready. This time before we leave out, I want the judge to swear you in, and this time we don't take the badged off."

"You three will be notified when your needed so make sure you have all of your gear ready to go at a moments notice, by the time this whole deal is settled you men will have quite a resume if you decide to pursue a profession as a law officer. I most certainly will not stand in your way, but also I will most certainly miss you gentlemen, but that's a day or two down the trail, so continue your duties and stay loose. "After saying this, the general opened the bottom drawer to his desk and pulled out a bottle and 2 cups and said, "I don't know about you, Hightower, every time I get around you. I end up with a shot of whiskey in my hand, or a weapon. You either have premonitions or you're just plain bad luck."

"A little bit of both, I guess general." For the next couple of hours the two men played checkers and drank whiskey, chased with black coffee. Hightower thought to himself about chasing whiskey with coffee, "chasing whiskey with coffee. What does that make a man? A sober drunk?"

The two men were interrupted when the door opened again, and the judge walked in. "I was sent to tell you that lunch is ready and you're expected to be there." "Well then I guess I had better show up or get another tongue lashing."

Getting up from his chair. Hightower shook the general's hand and made a fancy about-face, picked up his poncho and stepped out onto the boardwalk. The rain had not let up at all, and by now the compound was beginning to become a mudhole. Even though there had been drainage ditches and French drains put in the water was still standing and the Creek was just about to overflow its banks. Hightower was glad that the house been built on A small Hill, so the water would have to raise at least 15 or 20 feet before it would even become close to threatening the house. As the judge and Hightower walked back to the ranch house, the judge made the suggestion that they take their boots off on the porch before even trying to go into the house. Hightower agreed wholeheartedly.

Hightower just happened to look in the direction of Comanche and the horse was really enjoying standing in the rain. There were no flies on him, and the rain had washed all of the dust off of him and his coat was actually shiny will all of the water on him. The stallion would stand in the rain for a few minutes, then he would walk under a shelter that had been built and shake, throwing water everywhere and then he would go back out into the rain. He would jump and buck and run like he was a yearling. Hightower just smiled and then set down in a chair on the porch and took his boots off and his poncho and then he and the judge entered the house and instantly the smell of beef stew and cornbread came to Hightower and he told the judge, "I surely do hope we've got some buttermilk that's good and cold."

As Hightower and the judge entered the kitchen, Amy was standing looking out the window in the direction of the stockade and she said very solemnly, "there's something going on at the stockade, and it must be serious, because there's a whole troop of soldiers getting mounted and one of them is riding this way. " Hightower got up from the table and headed back to the front door. Just as he reached it the top Sgt. knocked and called Hightower's name. Barefoot with only socks on Hightower stepped out onto the porch and the top Sgt. saluted him and said, "the general sent me to get you sir, it appears somebody has hung an Indian and has also slaughtered on of your cattle. Being that the Indian was hung on reservation land and you a US Marshall, the general says it's your baby."

"Go ahead, you and the troop take off, I'll meet up with you in just a couple of minutes.", Hightower said. Stepping back inside the house Hightower grabbed his poncho and reached up on the wall and got down a Winchester, making sure it was loaded he then stepped back out on the porch and put his muddy boots back on. Rachel was standing in the doorway, watching every move that he made, and then she asked, "what's wrong. Edward? Where are you going? You haven't eaten your lunch yet"

"Keep it warm for me, sweetheart. I'll be back, just as soon as I can, don't worry, I just need to take a ride with the troop, " Then the top Sgt. spoke up saying, "I had Cpl Andrews saddle the big gray for you, he should be bringing the big gray here shortly, hope you don't mind? I just figured somebody that that big monster of a horse knew should be the one that saddle's him."

"Good idea top Sgt, that horse doesn't like just anybody, and he makes no bones about letting someone know that he doesn't like them. He on the other hand, likes Andrews, Lewis, and Mason. " The top Sgt. wheeled his horse and rode away, then motioning the troop to follow him. He turned and headed south West. As Hightower stood on the porch. Waiting for Andrews and Comanche he heard a sound behind him and instinctively spun, dropped to one knee, and drew his 45. Standing directly behind him was two troopers. One was a corporal and he spoke , saying, "the guard around your house has been doubled Sir, just wanted to let you know that there are two men on all four sides Of your house and they armed and ready. In your absence Sir, your house will be completely protected and everyone in it." "Who ordered this Cpl.?" Hightower ask. "When the patrol came in and told the general of the discovery of the Indian that was hanged, he issued the orders immediately Sir."

As Hightower turned he noticed Rachel standing in the doorway and she was carrying his double-barreled shotgun, and the look on her face said all that need to be said. She was dead serious about protecting her babies, her home, and her family. Hightower knew immediately that there was no sense in telling her to stay back, because his wife had been raised in church and with a believe in the Bible and if you ask her question about it, she'll tell you, "God helps those who help themselves."

He walked over and opened the screen door and with a smile he said to Rachel, " just make sure you know where your point that thing because it will make one hell of a big hole. That thing is loaded with double ought buck," then he gave her a for real kiss, not just a peck but a heart felt for real kiss and he said, "I can't love you anymore than I do right now, so I'm not going to tell you to be careful because I know you will. Don't stay in one place very long and for God's sake, keep that pretty head down."

When he turned around Andrews was there with the big gray and the big horse was anticipating a good run. He had his ears standing straight up, his nostrils were flared and he was pawing the ground with his right front foot, so Hightower said to the horse, "just hold on big boy, I've got a funny feeling you about to get all the exercise you can handle."

He placed the Winchester in it scabbard and swung into the saddle. Andrews took off after the troop, and the big gray immediately started following Andrews, but before long he was right beside him. It took about a half hour at a good steady gallop to find the spot where the beef had been slaughtered and the Indian had been hung. The troop had beat them there by about five minutes. As Hightower, dismounted the top Sgt. walked over to him and handed him a note that read, "I'm back Edward and I'll be seeing you soon." The note was unsigned, but Hightower knew who it was. Elizabeth Carter was very much alive, and hell bent on retaliation for the death of her son.

Hightower turned to Andrews and with ultimate of concern on his face said, "I really do hope that you three were dead serious when you said you were going to help me get rid of this problem. The one thing we wasn't counting on just happened, we're not going to have to find Elizabeth Carter, she's already found us. The only thing we don't know is how many men she has riding with her.

The chief of the Indians was standing there, so Hightower walked over to him and ask him in his native language, "will you send a tracker to find who done this. I don't want him to engaged them in any way, just let me know where they are." The chief gave a grunt and shook his head yes, then he turned and called the name of a certain brave. He then said. Just a few words to him and the brave swung up on the back of his pony and was gone with no question ask.

Hightower knew that Elizabeth Carter would head for the deepest and most secure place in the Bayou. So he needed the general to get in touch with his man who lives in the Bayou and tell him to keep his eyes and ears open and his mouth shut, but on the look out for Elizabeth Carter and her band of killers it finally dawned on Hightower what it was that Wade Jackson wanted to tell him. Elizabeth was alive and was headed his way with blood in her eyes. Climbing back aboard Comanche, and with Andrews right beside him. They headed back to the stockade and the general. All the way back. Hightower kept thinking how brazen Elizabeth was to come back to this part of the country. There was at least three murder warrants on her here, one count of escaping, and numerous warrants for bank robbery from other parts of the state. There was a warrant on her for the murder of Sheriff Caldwell in Las Cruces, New Mexico, and each bank robbery that she had been associated with at least one person had died at every one of the back robbers.

She had to be crazy, there was no other way to look at it. As they rode up in front of the general's office. There was quite a stir among the troopers, leading their horses into the barn they left them saddled and walked back and went into the general's office, he immediately sensed that there was something wrong when the general ordered everyone outside, except Hightower.

After everyone had left the general told Hightower to set down he had something to tell him. Then without beating around the bush he said, "the hanging of that Indian was a decoy and a maneuver to get as many troopers as possible away from the stockade. They attacked the house. Without any warning whatsoever the eight men guarding your house did everything they could top stop the marauders. Four of them died, but those eight men stood them off long enough for the men that was left at the stockade to go their defense." "My wife general, is she okay?" "Yes, Hightower, she's okay, but your mother-in-law and the judge, aren't. They were setting on the porch. When the first shots rang out, they never had a chance to even get out of their chairs. You can be proud of your wife and your sister-in-law their the reason no one entered the house. My men said they had never seen a woman load a shotgun so fast, both her and Dorothy fired at least three reloads of double ought buck. There are four troopers dead, but 11 of the marauders are lying face down in the mud."

Hightower jumped up out of his chair and hit the front door running, the mud was so slick that he fell twice before reaching the front porch. When he jumped up on the front porch the bodies of the judge and Amy were still lying there covered with ponchos. There were trooper everywhere standing guard. There were two troopers in the house, Lewis, and Mason, each man had a shotgun in one hand, two Army colts tucked in their belts, and one more colt in their other hand. It was a miracle that Hightower didn't get shot because he never broke stride when he entered the house. Muddy boots and all. Both of the troopers turned at the same time and two double barrel shotguns came to bare on Hightower, fortunately they recognized him and put the hammer's down. Lewis was the first to speak, "I'm sorry Hightower, we got here as quick as we possibly could, it was Elizabeth, I recognized her. They must have been hidden in that stand of trees over there," he pointed to a stand of oak trees and brush that had never been cleared. "When they attacked there was only two men on this side of the house, but it quickly became eight men, and they were firing with everything they had. Rachel and Dorothy both fired from the kitchen windows at the same time. They circled the house one time and then disappeared back through those trees. Rachel and Dorothy dropped one piece as they were riding off."

"where are they now,?" Hightower ask. "Their in that room right there with the babies and both dogs, I believe they still have two shotguns and a box of shells a piece, I don't know for sure, and there ain't no way in hell I'm knocking on that door."!!

"Can you get a few men to get Mr. and Mrs. Tatum off of the front porch, I guess the best place to lay them out would be in the bunkhouse I'm quite sure that the undertaker from town would find it a lot easier to get them from there than from their bedroom upstairs. Now stand back, Lewis, I'm going to try to get Rachel and Dorothy to open that door." Lying down on the floor and as flat on the floor as he possibly could get he reached up, knocked on the door with one hand and said, "Rachel, Dorothy, it's me Edward, for God sakes don't shoot."

The door opened very slowly until he could see Rachel, peeking through the crack and then the door swung open. She was still carrying the shotgun and Dorothy was standing in front of the babies cribs, and both dogs were standing in front of her with their ears laid back and their teeth showing. When they seen Hightower their tails started wagging and they turned back to the cribs and smelled the babies to make sure they were okay, then they lay down in their normal places on guard once again.

Having gotten up off of the floor. He took the shotgun from Rachel and handed it to Lewis and told him to hang it back on the wall. Rachel was still shaking and she was scared, but not scared enough to run and hide. Hightower put his arms around her and motioned for Dorothy to join them. Hightower put his arms around the women and just held them for a few moments, then Dorothy leaned back and looked at Hightower and said, "Edward, they killed mom and dad, they shot them down in cold blood, they never had a chance." "I know Dorothy, and I promise both you and Rachel that I will personally either hang Elizabeth Carter, or bury her. The babies are they okay?"

Rachel answered, "yes their all right Edward, and I must tell you that those two puppies never left the babies sides. They stated right there as close to them as they could get, and they were ready to fight. They were even protecting Dorothy and I and I can absolutely say they meant business."

Mason walked through the door over the Dorothy and asked her for her shotgun. He then broke it down and look the two empty shells out of it. She had been so excited after the last time she fired as the marauders were riding away, she had forgot to reload. From behind him. He heard Lewis say, "well I'll be damned," turning Hightower asked Lewis what was wrong. Lewis's answer was, "this shotgun has empty shells in it too."

Walking out into the living room Hightower seen the general standing there and ask, "can you send somebody into town to get the undertaker to come out to get the judge and Amy?" "I'll do better that that Edward, I'll have them loaded on the buckboard and I'll send a detachment along with them to town." "Two men on the buckboard and two men escorting it should be enough general. The last thing I want to do is take a bunch of troopers away from this outpost. Know Elizabeth the way I do, she's probably out there somewhere watching and waiting for another chance, she won't stop general."

General Whitehead stood silent for just a moment and then he said, "until this is over, Edward, I want to move Rachel and both babies, Dorothy, and the dogs to the stockade. I can move the officers into the bunkhouse and the ladies into their living quarters."

Then the anger came out in Rachel and she said, "this is my home, and Elizabeth Carter, that bitch is not going to force me out of it. Thank you for the thoughts general, but I am staying right here where I belong." "That goes for me to general, Dorothy said. We can't let that woman win."

Lewis came back into the living room and said, "Sir, we are all loaded and ready to go." Rachel ask, "can I see them before you take them to town?" The general looked at Rachel and said very softly, "of course you can, Rachel, but I don't think it's a good idea for you to see all of that blood, and it's my understanding that your mother was shot in the face, your father, well, you just shouldn't see him, yet. Edward, can I speak to you out on the porch for just a minute, The general asked?"

The two men walked out onto the porch and the general told Hightower, "I have wired for a another squad and they should be here sometime tomorrow, I'm going to beef up the security around here. Four good men were killed and that makes your problem, my problem. What ever you need, it's yours. I want this woman's head on a stick, do you understand me, Mr. Hightower?" "Yes Sir, I believe I do. What I need is information and Andrews, Lewis, and Mason." Hightower turned to walk back in the house. Then he stopped and said, "there's one thing more general, I would like to have Andrews, Lewis, and Mason here in the house just as a precaution, I know there's going to be troopers outside, but I would still ask that these three men be station inside the house."

"Like I said, Edward what ever you need, you got it."

The general hollered at Lewis and said, "find someone to take your place on that buckboard you're staying here, notify Andrews and Mason to report to me here." When Hightower walked back into the house, he found Rachel and Dorothy holding the babied and being accompanied by King and Josie. Both women's eyes were swelled from crying, but they were determined to make the best out of the worst.

Hightower walked over the liquor cabinet, picked up a glass and started to pour some whiskey. But then he stopped, he set the glass down put the cork back in the bottle and put it back in the cabinet and then he asked Rachel, "I'm going to be up for quite a while tonight, do you think one of you ladies could put on a pot of coffee?" Without saying anything. Rachel laid Rebecca down on the blanket next to King and got up and headed for the kitchen. Dorothy laid Junior on the blanket next to Josie and stood up saying, "I'll be right back. I'm going to help Rachel. Edward, she hasn't eaten all day, you need to make her eat, if you don't, she's going to get sick, and that's going to be bad for these babies."

"You fix her something Dorothy, and I'll make damn sure she eats it, okay?. As a matter of fact, I can eat a little bit of that beef stew, I never did get any at lunch. If you heat up two bowls and I'll make sure Rachel eats. Has she fed the babies yet" She was in the process when all hell broke loose. I don't know if she has ever finished feeding them or not, if you want, I'll ask her." "That might be a good idea Dorothy, Hightower said but do it gently." Then Hightower looked at Dorothy and ask her, " Are you alright Dorothy?" She looked at Hightower and said, "no, but I will be when that bitch is dead. Right now the only thing I'm worried about is my sister, and those two babies in there on that blanket." "You and me both Hightower said" "she's too quiet and I'm afraid she's going to be like a volcano. When it does come out. She may below the top of her head, keep an eye on her Dorothy, please." "You don't worry about Rachael I'll take care of her, you just make that bitch pay!!!"

Hightower walked back out and set down on the porch and listened to the rain and thought how he was going to end this , as he sat there pondering his next move. He glanced up and there was a lone rider coming up the road riding very slowly on a buckskin horse wearing a black slicker and his head was bowed forward to keep the rain out of his face. A couple of the troopers wearing slickers stopped him for just a second and then pointed to the house and let the man ride on. Hightower didn't recognize him till he pulled up in front of the house and he said, "looks like I'm a little too late. I apologize for that, what happened here Edward?" All hell broke loose Wade, there's no wondering if she's alive or where she is anymore." Then Hightower turned to one of the troopers and said, "take Mr. Jackson's horst to the barn, unsaddled him and dry him off, then feed him and water him, oh hell trooper just take care of him, please."

Then, Hightower got up from his seat and motion for Wade to follow him inside. As they entered the house. Rachel, who had come back and set down in the floor with the babies got up and with the grace of the lady that she was with a big smile, she said, "Mr. Jackson, here let me take that wet poncho." Then she turned and told Dorothy to pour 2 cups of coffee and then she sad, "come out and meet one of Edwards longest and dearest friends." Dorothy came into the living room and stuck out her hand and said, "I remember Mr. Jackson from the wedding, you know, the one you couldn't make because you went into labor." Wade took his hat off and took Dorothy's hand and said, "it's good to see you again, miss Dorothy, when you told me that Rachel was not in the shape to travel, I thought maybe she just didn't want to come to the wedding," looking down at the twins laying on the blanket Wade, smiled and let out a short laugh and continued by saying, "I don't reckon she was up to traveling. How old are they now?" "Not quite a year old yet, Dorothy said,"

"Would you like a shot of whiskey to go with that coffee Wade?, it'll get the chill out of your bones." "That sounds like a might good idea Edward. A shot of whiskey and a good hot cup of coffee will hit the spot. Edward, when the Las Cruces Sheriff went through the ashes of the burned our ranch house, where the Carter gang made their last stand. All they found was a tunnel that had been erected in the basement that went for some hundred yards, and came out below the horizon behind the house. There were tracks that proved two people had escaped. Later It had been said that Elizabeth Carter had been seen in a place called red stone Arizona, but when the Marshall's arrives there, she was long gone. Not long after that, another gang started robbing banks and the thing that scares the hell out of everybody is that the gang is being led by a woman who cares nothing about killing innocent people. We now know it's Elizabeth Carter and I have been directed to give you these orders from the attorney general, "bring her in Dead or Alive"!!......... You're really the only person that knows what she looks like, I can tell you this much Edward, she's not using Lily Barnes as a name anymore, she's being extremely brazen because she went back to her original name Elizabeth Carter and she wants everybody to know that she is still out there and still just as dangerous. There has been a string of bank robberies from Tucson following the border all the way around to Brownsville. I guess she figured they had enough money for right now because that's where the back robbery stopped, but there is a trail of dead law man leading from Brownsville all the way over to Lake Charles, Louisiana. And now she has added the death of a federal judge and his wife to her resume. I've been directed to make sure you get all of the help you need. So if you need it. You ask for it and you'll get it, that's my word to you. Edward and my promise."

"I've got a few of the Indians tracking Elizabeth and what's left of her gang. Hightower said, I'm quite sure that they're going to head for the Bayou again but this time it won't hide them. I made the mistake the last time of not going into the Bayou after her, I won't make that same mistake twice. This time it's not my job, this time it's personal and I won't stop."

"Well, if there's anything I can do to help you, just give me a holler, Wade said". Setting his empty coffee cup down and his whiskey glass. Wade stood up and once again offered his condolences to Rachel and Dorothy telling them that he was sorry for their loss. Then he turned to Hightower stuck out his hand and as the two men shook hands, there wasn't any words said, but the looks on both men's faces spoke volumes. Elizabeth Carter was a dead woman, she just hadn't laid down yet.

The two men walked out onto the porch. Wade asked Lewis, "if you don't mind, would you go get my horse for me, I need to be getting back toward Tyler. I've got a family feud going on over there and so far nobody has been killed, but it's going to happen, and when it does I had best be right in the middle. If things keep going the way they are Edward, we're going to need a whole lot more lawmen, we don't have near enough law men the way that Texas is growing. Other than a few town or country Sheriff's, the only law in Texas is us and the Rangers. Maybe one day the politicians will get smart enough to hire more men, but I doubt it, they ain't done nothing extremely smart yet."

The rain had slacked off slightly, so when Lewis got to the porch with Wade's horse. Wade dawned his poncho and swung into the saddle so that the seat would not get wet and once again said goodbye and turned the buckskin West headed for Tyler and home. Hightower looked at one of the troopers that were guarding the front porch and asked him if he get someone to bring a bucket of how soapy water and a scrub brush and removed the blood from the front porch. "Yes Sir, the trooper said. I'll take care of it right away, Sir."

Lewis looked over at Hightower and said, "I'm going to take a spin around the house and check on all the troopers. And make sure that their alert and ready to fight. Just in case." Hightower nodded his head yes, saying, "that's a good idea, Lewis, thanks."

Hightower turned and walked back into the house, Rachel and Dorothy were not in the living room with the babies and the dogs were gone to, so he walked back to the bedroom the door was open, so he peaked in and lying there on the bed with the babies between them was Rachel and Dorothy. King was lying on the floor next to Rachel, and Josie was lying on the floor next to Dorothy. It was a picture of complete serenity as all four Rachel, Junior, Becky, and Dorothy were asleep, the dogs were only cat napping because the minute. Hightower appeared in the doorway both dogs stood up till they seen who it was then they laid back down, content that things were okay.

Not feeling that he could lay down and actually go to sleep. Hightower very quietly turned around and went back out on the porch being careful not to set in the light coming from the windows of the house and keeping his Winchester close at hand. He had forgotten about the two troopers who were guarding the front porch of which one of them was Lewis. Hightower had just sit down and leaned back when Lewis spoke, "is something wrong Hightower?" Springing to his feet and cocking the Winchester suddenly Lewis said in a very distinctive voice , "don't shoot I'm on your side, besides, I'm over here." Stepping into the light where Hightower could see him jokingly Lewis said, "you would have shot the hell out of something, but it wasn't going to be me. You were a good 5 feet off."

"Thanks Lewis, I guess I better get my head on straight, but I can't seem to get my mind off of the judge and Amy. The house already seems to quiet and a lot bigger than it used to be. Those two people are going to be missed not only by this family, but by the people of Lake Charles they were staples in the community constantly helping people and defending those who needed it. I know that Rachel and Dorothy has cried a lot, but I don't think the full impact of their mom and dad being gone has hit them as hard as it should have. That means the worst is yet to come, and I dread it."

"I don't think we should wait, I think we should go after them murdering sons of bitches and deal out to them the justice they deserve. Lewis Said". Hightower knew Lewis was right, but right at this time he could not leave Rachel and the babies or Dorothy, maybe after the funerals, but not now.

You stay close Lewis and stay alert. I think I'm going to take me a walk down to the barn and spend some time with Comanche, he hasn't been rubbed down or talked to in a long time, he likes that." Then Hightower stepped off of the porch and vanished into the shadows. Lewis spoke very softly saying, "trooper stay out of the window light and stay alert, it's going to be a long night. If you start feeling yourself getting sleepy there's a pot of coffee on the kitchen stove and cups are right next to the pot. If you need sugar, It's on the kitchen table, sorry no milk for your coffee. Is Andrews and Mason in the house?" "Yeah Cpl. Mason is sitting next to the back door and Andrews is setting in the corner right behind you, both men won't be seen until your close enough for them to knocked you down."

Knowing that the rest of the men would be relieved in just a little over an hour Lewis settled back into the darkness, and waited for any sound that didn't belong. He himself would miss the judge and his sense of humor and his knowledge of life, he would miss Amy and the smile that was always on her face her tenderness that extended past her family to strangers and her willingness to help any person that needed it , and he would especially miss her cooking, That reminded him, she never did get to prepare a meal for Mr. Dean like she promised, but he felt sure that Mr. Dean would understand.

Lewis was setting as quiet as he possibly could, when he heard a sound coming from just off of the porch to the left. Knowing that Hightower was out there, but not knowing if it was him or not. Lewis was not inclined to give away his position just in case. So very quietly he hunkered down with his 45 in his hand, simply because it was easier to manage in close quarters. The sound came again, and Lewis got prepared, then he seen the outline of a man, and he dove off of the porch with as much force as he could muster and aimed his body at the outline and on the impact of the two bodies coming together. Lewis heard his top Sgt.'s voice saying, "damn trooper, are you trying to cripple somebody."

Lewis figured he was in trouble, but instead the top Sgt. got up from the ground and patted him on the shoulder and said" good job Lewis, that was using your head and I'm glad you did, because anybody else would have probably shot me. Your relief is right behind me, brief them on what their duties are and where the best place is to stand their post." "When I'm relieved Sir, if it's all right with you I'll step inside, and join Andrews and

Mason. If there's three of us in there. That means that one can sleep for a couple of hours and then relieve one of the others letting him sleep for a couple of hours and we can keep going that till daylight, but I really do think besides the troopers on the front and back porch and along the sides of the house that there should be at least three troopers in the house at all times."

The top Sgt. scratched his head, "sounds good to me, he said, but let me run it by the general okay.? Anyway, you have my permission to join Andrews and Mason inside, I don't think I have to tell you dim all the lights and don't get between the lights and the Windows at any time."

The top Sgt. turned to leave, and there on the porch setting in a chair was Hightower, "that was good advice top Sgt. It's just too bad that both of you are dead. If I had been an outlaw. This house would have been compromised." Lewis looked at the other end of the porch and said, "trooper where are you,?" "I'm dead too Cpl, I never heard a thing until Mr. Hightower put his hand over my mouth and his finger in my back, I'll swear I believe that he is part Indian, I can't believe I didn't hear anything, no rustling of the leaves no squishing of the wet ground, nothing, I heard nothing." "The reason you didn't hear anything trooper was because you were distracted by Lewis and the top Sgt., your focus on the night had been removed by their actions."

Hightower had been gone, the better part of two hours, he had spent about 30 minutes with Comanche, and the rest of that time he had taken his moccasins out of his saddlebags that were still hanging on the door of the stall where Comanche was and put them on, then preceded to make a wide swing around the ranch house, including down into the clump of trees that Elizabeth and her gang came out of to start with. There was no doubt about it, Elizabeth and her gang had headed in the direction of the Bayou. Even if they embedded themselves deep into the Bayou sooner or later they would have to come out to buy such things as flour, meal, salt, and pepper, coffee, and tobacco. If they tried to hold up for very long in the Bayou they would be trapped.

There needs to be people keeping an eye out for them, and when they are sited they need to be spied on constantly. If they try to move the ideal place to catch them is in the desert due West of St. Charles. If they make it past Beaumont and Galveston, they'll make it to the Mexican border. They mustn't be allowed to get off into the Bayou, they may continue along and try to get into the other section of Bayou Northeast of New Orleans. But unless they split up they would be noticed, the only other way to disappear would be to go to Lake Charles and all of them get on ship headed to any place along the Mexican Border, where they wouldn't have to hide. Then Hightower muttered to himself, "I should have shot that bitch years ago, if I had I wouldn't be chasing her around like trying to catch a wild pig."

Chapter 4

Without meaning to, Hightower spent the rest of the night asleep sitting in a chair in the living room with a sawed off double barrel 12 gauge shotgun lying across his lap and a Winchester leaned up against his leg, and needless to say, no one in the house had the nerve to wake him up, even when he started talking in his sleep about what needed to happen to Elizabeth Carter and every member of her gang.

When Rachel woke up the next morning, and after she had changed both babies and fed them. She then brought them into living room and laid them down on the blanket so they could play, no one but Rachel dared to wake up Hightower. Rachel just giggled and said, "it's not who wakes him up, it's how you wake him up. Here let me show you." She then walked over and very gently sat down on the arm of the chair and leaned over and blew her warm breath into his ear very gently, and when Hightower opened his eyes he was looking into the face of his wife. The shotgun was moved away from Rachel so was the Winchester. There was no tension on his face, that had been replaced with a look of kindness and love. He reached up to kiss Rachel and it finally dawned on him where he was. Looking around he seen the smiling faces of Andrews, Lewis, and Mason. Andrews looked at Rachel and with a big smile on his face and said, "Mrs. Hightower, if that is the only way to wake him up without getting shot, then I guess I'll just have to get shot because I'm not kissing that big ugly mug."!!!…. This brought a round of laughter from the men on the front porch, who had been watching what was going on, and of course Dorothy was laughing and somewhere down the line Mason said that he even thought the dogs had laughed too.

Then the reality that Mr. and Mrs. Tatum was not there struck everyone as if they had been slapped in the face. Then the tears welled up in Rachel and Dorothy's eyes and it was what Hightower had been waiting for both of the young women fell apart, Dorothy turned to Mason and he didn't say a word. He just stuck out his arms and she clung to him as tight as she could Rachel slid off of the arm of the chair on to Hightower's lap, and her tears within moments had the front of Hightower shirt soaking wet. Everyone else turned their backs not so much to give Hightower and Rachel, Mason and Dorothy privacy, but to keep them from seeing the tears roll down the faces of these hard-boiled war toughened troopers.

Finally, Hightower took his handkerchief and wiped Rachel's eyes and then he said to her, with the voice filled with love, "sweetheart, your mom and dad are not here in body, but they are in spirit and they always will be here looking over you, Dorothy, and the grandbabies. I know it seems to you that there is no way the pain will ever stop, but it will Rachel. The loving memories that you have of your mom and dad will never go away, but the pain will. You'll stop remembering the day they were taken away from you, the time will come when you will remember only the laughter that filled this house, the love that your mom and dad gave you everyday day, and the fact that your father and your mother were extremely proud of both of their daughters. The only thing that I can tell you Rachel, and you too Dorothy, to help with your pain is ask yourself what would The Honorable Judge Welter Tatum and his loving wife Amy Rose Tatum do in a situation like this?. Me, I choose to believe that both of them would stand up tall and I can hear the judge say, "what has happened just isn't right, but by gum, it's up to us to set it straight. You get these people in the courthouse in front of me and I'll take care of the rest."!!!

Rachel straightened up and placed a hand on each side of Hightower's face and said, "someday I want you to introduce me to the Indian who put that arrow in your back. Without that arrow I would have never met you, Edward Hightower." Then she took Hightower's handkerchief, wiped her eyes, then blew her nose on it and said, "come on Dorothy, crying is not going to help. Edward is right mom and dad wouldn't cry, they would get mad and as dad would say, "Hells a comin, and heads are going to roll. I'm pretty sure Dorothy that we've got some hungry men who could use a good breakfast and a good hot cup of coffee, how about it's sis?"

Dorothy backed up from Mason and wiped her eyes on his shirt sleeve and then with a look of determination in her eyes and on her face she said, "let's go see just how much we've learned from Mama." With that being said, the two women disappeared into the kitchen and it sounded just the same as it did when Amy was in there with them. Hightower leaned back in his chair, stretched, and then he preceded to get down on the floor and play with his son and his daughter. Soon the laughter of the two children could be heard throughout the house and conversation could be heard coming from kitchen and the sound made everything seem that it was just the same today as it was yesterday, and what made things really seem right is, in his heart Hightower knew that tomorrow would be even better.

Outside on the front porch there was a changing of the guards, the sun was starting to peek over the Eastern horizon, and it was then that Hightower realized that it had stopped raining and the higher the sun got, the more he could tell that it was going to be a clear, warm, day.

Hightower walked over to Mason and as he started to walk by him, he put his right hand on Mason's shoulder and said, "I think that you have got some thinking to do, it seems that you have been chosen to become a member of this family. Let me know what you and Dorothy decide because this house deserves to have the sound of people's laughter in it again, and this ranch deserves to be called home. We'll talk after a while about the future, but as of now I'm after a good hot steaming cup of coffee how about you, "Mr. Mason?"

Just about that time there came a knock on the front door, Andrews opened the door, it was the general. Hightower stepped up and said, be bashful general, come on in. You're just in time for a good cup of coffee and in just a little bit will have breakfast, and you're more than welcome to join us."

"That's a mighty tempting offer, the general said, but didn't come here for breakfast, and I don't know if this is the right time for this or not, but it needs to be taken care of. The undertaker has scheduled Mr. and Mrs. Tatum's funeral for this afternoon. He said to tell you that he had taken extra care in the preparation of both of the Tatum's. The funeral wagon will be escorted by full squads of troopers, and I'm personally going to lead the troopers. I think it would be the right thing to do if you four men carried the coffins of both the Tatum's, but that's up to you." Hightower studied for a moment and then asked the general, "can you spare four men as pallbearers? If you can then I'll use two of your men along with me and Mason to carry the judge. And the other two men can join Andrews and Lewis carrying miss Amy, Rachel will walk along in front of her father and Dorothy will walk along in front of her mother. That way we can carry both of them at the same time making no difference between them."

The general very reluctantly called Rachel and Dorothy's names, and when they appeared from the kitchen, he asked, "did you ladies happen to hear what we have planned for your mom and dad's funeral?" Dorothy spoke up and said, "yes, we heard and what ever Edward decides is fine with us."

Asked the general turned and started for the door he paused and said, "I am going to double the security around your house while were gone, and l am going to put my best men on it. I don't want you to worry about your place it will take an act of God to do anything to this house. I think we should leave here no later than noon tomorrow, that will put us in town about one or maybe a little after. I'm quite sure there's going to be quite a few people at the funeral, and I have designated certain men to keep an eye on "everyone" at the funeral I believe that she may have men sneak into town to see who they hit. Any strangers will be corralled and questioned, we just might get lucky Edward."

With a tip of his hat the general was out the door and talking to the top Sgt. saying, "I want either an officer or a Sgt. in charge of each two-hour session of guard duty. And I want the best we have standing these post, do you understand me top Sgt.?" "Yes Sir, I'll see to it." Giving a salute to the general the top Sgt. was off down across the compound and with every step he took he hollered a troopers name.

By the time he had reached the mess Hall there was a string of noncommissioned officers and two second lieutenants, and one first Lieut. the top Sgt. signaled for everyone together around. Then he said, "during the day there will be four men standing guard on the house. One front, one back, and one on each side of the house, after dark. The sentries will double and you will walk a roving patrol for two hours, and then eight more men and one officer will take over the next shift. This will continue from dusk till Dawn. Remember above all, there are four people in that house who must be protected at all cost in case any of you are not familiar with who I'm talking about. They are, Rachel Hightower, Dorothy Tatum, Edward Hightower Junior, and last but not least Rebecca Marie Hightower. You are hereby charged with the absolute safety of these two women and the two children. Do you have any questions,? If so speak up now? If you officers and noncoms have no questions, then pick your eight men and stand by."!!!

Then the top Sgt. seen Hightower standing on the porch and he asked in a loud voice, "do you, Mr. Hightower have anything to add?" "No", Hightower said, "just be safe and stay alert, me and my family thanks you for keeping them safe".

Turning and going back through the front door. He was met by Dorothy carrying a plate of cat head biscuits with sausage or ham. She had already taken care of the two troopers on the back porch, now, the two troopers on the front porch had a cat head biscuits in each hand and she told them she would be back with a cup of coffee in just a minute. Andrews, Lewis, and Mason were seated at the kitchen table with their weapons lying on the table within easy reach. Rachel said to Hightower, "I told them to sit down and eat the breakfast, but they refused because they were on guard duty, so we compromised. They are still on guard duty, but they can eat their breakfast at the same time. Now you." Edward Hightower." set down and eat your breakfast."!

It seemed as though Rachel had reverted back to her old self with a touch of her Mama, so Hightower simply sit down and shut up and had the feeling that Rachel Hightower was a lot stronger than he had ever seen. His wife was a fighter and this very moment she was proving it, and incidentally, so was her sister.

When breakfast was over with. Hightower decided he was going down and see the chief and find out if the brave. He sent after Carter and her gang had determined where they were headed. After telling Rachel what he intended to do, she simply kissed him on the cheek and said, "you go do what you have to do to bring her in. You don't worry about us we'll be fine," then she kissed him again, this time on the lips, and when he turned to go. She smacked him on the butt and said, "supper will be at six, don't be late."!

Tomorrow was going to be a very rough day for Rachel and Dorothy. This would be the first time in their lived that they had ever been separated from their parents and sooner or later it would dawn on them that they would never see them again, and until that happened. Neither one of the girls would ever be the same again. What Hightower did not want to happen was for Rachel and Dorothy to both become distant, withdrawn and cold in feelings, to build a shell around their hearts trying to protect themselves from any more pain. Maybe the twins can help draw them out. Anyway, all anyone could do was wait and see.

On the way down to the corral to get Comanche, he was met by general Whitehead, who in turn asked where he was going. Hightower explained that he was going to see the chief and the general said, "I've been meaning to go see the chief myself mind if I ride along with you?" "Don't mind at all general as a matter of fact, I'd enjoy the company." As they neared the barn a trooper met them, leading both horses which were already saddled. The trooper had a great big smile on his faces and said, "I seen you two gentlemen walking toward the barn and I figured that you were going for a ride so just taking a chance I saddle both horses for you. I sure do hope I didn't mess up general."

The general laid his hand on the old troopers shoulder and said, "Johnson, you have been able to read me like a book ever since the first time we met, I don't think that you could ever make a mistake unless you planned to." "Aw I make mistakes Sir, it's just that I've lived long enough to figure out how to cover them up."

Hightower looked at the timer and ask, "just how old are you Trooper?" The trooper looked at Hightower and scratched his head. Then said, "my Paw said I was 16 when I joined the cavalry, if that's true. I've been in the cavalry, Sir, for 50 years come my next birthday." "Don't you think it's about time you retired Hightower ask." "No, Sir this man's army is the only life I've ever known, and besides there ain't no place that I can go that I ain't already been. Ain't ever been one to lick my wounds twice, when die I want to be in uniform and with my boots on."

Hightower, smiled at the old trooper and said, "with an attitude like that trooper I would say that you will probably outlive me, The general, and most of the troopers that are assigned to this post. Besides, none of us can afford to lose you, as much as you have seen, and as many things that you have done. You can remind us of the mistakes that we made in the past and keep us from making the same mistakes again."

Climbing aboard Comanche, and with the general at his side. Hightower headed Southwest to the camp of the Cherokee Indians who this new reservation was set up for. And by federal law was under the protection of general Whitehead and his men. Hightower being a federal marshals was the only law man in the neighborhood who had the authority to go on to the reservation without asking permission, but respecting the Indians the way Hightower did he would never do that unless it was extremely urgent or to catch a killer.

The general and Hightower Road at a pretty good gallop for over an hour. Then as they topped a small rise, they seen the Indians encampment. Immediately they were met by a band of Braves, who said, "why are you here?" Hightower answered them in their native tongue, "we seek to see you here?" we come in peace with no ill our heart." The Indian who spoke first said, "you speak are tongue very well, are you the law man Hightower?" "Yes, I am Hightower." "Then come, follow me" then he and the other Braves turned their Horses toward the encampment and rode off at an easy pace. There were three Indians in front of the general and Hightower, and three behind them.

The general looked a little uneasy. So Hightower said to him, "don't look so worried general, we are getting the royal treatment by being led into the encampment still wearing our guns is a mark of friendship. To the Indians we are the same as Chiefs of another tribe, but just to keep things friendly do not at any time attempt to touch your weapon, or draw your sword. One more thing, don't sit until the chief sits."

As the two men rode into the camp. Hightower noticed that there were more women than men, and that worried him. There were also numerous children and it looked as if each living structure also had a dog. Whether it was for protection, or being a pet for the children. He didn't know, but he would soon find out. Swinging down off of Comanches back. Hightower put his right hand over his heart and then Palm down. Let his am point to the chief which to Hightower's understanding was a sign of friendship, at least it was to the Comanche he wasn't quite sure what it meant to the Cherokee, but it couldn't be anything bad.

The chief spoke some English, so when Hightower would ask a question the chief would try to answer in English, if he couldn't find the words. Then he would answer in Cherokee. But before Hightower could get around to answering any questions he and the general had to smoke the peace pipe, which didn't have tobacco in it, he wasn't real sure what was in it, but it wasn't tobacco maybe it was ragweed anyway, It tasted bad. The general stood up. Shaking his head no and pointing at the pipe, then he went over to his saddlebags and reached in and brought out two pretty good size bags of tobacco. Cleaning out the pipe he put the real tobacco in and handed it back to the chief along with the two bags. The medicine man, then lit the pipe for the chief, and after talking a good puff on it. The chief smiled and pass it back to the general. With a nod of his head, he took the pipe and standing up. Once again, he pointed the pipe to the East, and then to the West and then talking a good long puff he handed it to Hightower, who did the same." For the next 15 or 20 minutes. There was a dialogue of pleasant stories passed back and forth between the chief, the general, and Hightower.

The chief evidently has something else to do, because finally he said, "Hightower, why are you here? Are you here to find out where those who killed the judge and his wife has gone?" Never moving his eyes from the chief's face, Hightower nodded his head yes and then said, "it is extremely important that I find out where they are, or at least what direction they went away in. "Cannot tell you're going to have to get your man in the Bayou busy. We have got to returned yet, maybe before the next moon."

Hightower looked at the general and said, "well, that settles it general, you're going to have to get your man in the Bayou busy. We have got to know what direction Carter and what's left of her gang went. Your troopers dropped 11 of her men, and I would say it's possible that two or three others were wounded, so can you check around and see if any doctor within a 50 mile radius has gone missing since the raid on the ranch."

Standing up the general spoke to the chief in a very fluent Cherokee tongue, "as soon as you hear from your Braves no matter what time day or night you send a rider to get in touch with me. I must know where this evil woman and her band of evil men has gone. They must be punished not only for the death of the judge and his wife. But for the death of your young brave that they hung for no reason." Then as Hightower stood up, he asked the chief, "do you have meat to feed you people? If you do not let me know and I will send you a beef and I will personally escort you off of the reservation to go on a hunt to prepare your people for winter."

The chief stood up and in broken English said, "Hightower friend. Hightower fight Indian. But always treat Indian with respect. My people will do everything they can to find this evil woman." Then in the white man's custom the chief stuck out his hand, first to general, then to Hightower. Then as the two men started to get on their horses the medicine man walked up and shook some kind of a rattle and said sentence that they didn't understand, so looking back at the chief Hightower ask, "what did you medicine man, just say?" "Medicine man say, good spirit ride with you and protect you, for from this day on both white eyes are friend of Cherokee."

Getting back on their horses and leaving the camp at a slow walk the general asked. Hightower, "have you noticed that there is not very many men in this encampment?" "Yes, I have general and I think I know why. I heard some of the younger men talking while you were talking to the chief, it seems that a young brave that was hanged is one of the chiefs sons, so I've would venture to say right now that the braves who are missing are on the trail of Elizabeth Carter and they have gotten revenge on their minds and blood in their eyes. We have to But it might not be a bad idea to have them on our side. When we do run into them. Wouldn't that be a kick in the head general, white man, and Indians working together to bring in a bunch of killers. What do you think the people would have to say about that?"

"It would be a glorious day, Mr. Hightower, and it would do away with a lot of bitter feelings about granting this land as a reservation to the Indians. Personally I think it would be better for the Indians and for the people if they were to allow the Cherokees to go back to their lands in North Carolina, South Carolina, Virginia. Have you ever been in the great Smoky Mountains Edward? If you haven't then it's a trip that you should take your wife on its beautiful country and white man, and Indians work together there. Did you know, Mr. Hightower that a lot of young Eastern men, has taken Cherokee women for brides, why in 10 or 12 years. I really don't believe that there will be a full-blooded Englishman or a full-blooded anything on the East Coast. It's my understanding, Mr. Hightower that somewhere down the line in your family there's Indian blood."

"Yes Sir, there is my great-grandmother was a Chippewa, and all of my dad's people tell me that she was an extremely beautiful woman, maybe that's where I get my good looks."

That brought out a resounding round of laughter from the general and then he said, "seems to me that you got the short end of the stick, Mr. Hightower." Then there was another round of laughter not only from the general but from Hightower.

All the way back to the ranch, the two men looked for signs hoping that they would run across the trail that Carter and her men left when they left the ranch. They couldn't have covered their trail. They were traveling too fast, I'd say that they were anticipating a troop of United States cavalry bearing down on them, but it didn't happen, and that fact would undoubtedly put a heap more trouble on Hightower.

When they rode into the compound and up to the barn, they were met by the old trooper who ask, "general, Sir, are you and Mr. Hightower going out again? If you are, I'll just loosen the saddles, if you aren't I'll take him off and rub him down and give them some grub."

The general looked at Hightower and said, "I can't speak for Mr. Hightower, but I'm not going back out anytime soon." "Neither am I Hightower said. I think I'm going to spend the rest of the day with my wife and the twins, if those two ferocious dogs, I've got will let me close to them." The old timer smiled and said, "the only way those two puppies would ever hurt anybody is if they tried to hurt those babies, them are two of the best behaved dogs I gave ever seen. Did you know, Sir, that they pay me a visit every morning and we have a cup of coffee and some beef jerky together. Hell, they even shake hands with me."!

Climbing down off of Comanche, Hightower patted him on the neck rubbed him on the face and massaged his ears all the time and talking to him and showing him all the kindness and love that he could muster. Finally, the old trooper led the stallion into the barn and as Hightower walked away, he could hear the old timer carrying on a conversation with Comanche.

When he walked into the house, the three troopers were still there, and they were ready for anything that came their way. Andrews was seated by the window in the front of the house, next to him was two Winchesters, one double-barreled 12gauge shotgun.

Lewis was seated next to a window in the dining room with the same array of weapons. Mason was seated strategically where he could see out the back door without being seen from outside, heat too had two Winchesters, one 12gauge shotgun, plus, he carried two 45 colt's.

Hightower thought to himself, "someone would have to be totally crazy to try and force their way into this house, it would be just plain stupid."

Before he could get to the kitchen, Rachel met him with her arms wide open, jumping into his waiting arms and while giving him a big hug and a kiss and she said, "I am so glad you're back home, I have missed you terribly all day. Beside you missed lunch, come on in and I'll fix you a bowl of some of the best beef stew I have ever fixed. I got Mama's recipe Book out and there is a lot of good recipes in that book.

As he walked by the door to the bedroom he noticed Dorothy lying on the bed playing with the babies and when she seen him a big smile came a crossed her face as she raised up her hand in the waving motion and then continued playing with the kids. Hightower paused for just a moment to listen to the giggles in the squeals of the two babies and evidently the dogs sensed that there was no harm that could befall the twins because they were lying in the bedroom doorway facing out into the hall and watching every move that he made. Being accepted by these two dogs meant that he was not trusted, so he leaned down and patted each puppy on the head and told them how good a job they were doing. Hightower didn't believe that they understood him, but they sure acted like they did.

Meanwhile Rachel hollered at the three troopers in the house and told them to come and eat some lunch. Then she went to the back door where the second lieutenant was standing and told him to let half of his men go to lunch, and when they got back the other half could go to lunch. The second lieutenant started to say something, but when Rachel pointed her finger at him, he just simply said, "yes ma'am"!

Andrew spoke up and said, "Hightower, those two women have been like a couple of bee's buzzing around, Rachel took care of your suit that she intends for you to wear to the funeral tomorrow, while Dorothy washed and ironed dry the dresses that they're going to wear. They even have our uniform ready for us to wear. Rachel told us that it was all spit and polish, if we were going to carry her mom and dad to their final resting place, it would be with the ultimate of class." "You didn't by any chance try to argue with her, did you?" "Absolutely not, do I look like an idiot. That woman would have taken a broom to me, or worse If I had tried to oppose her in any way, no sirree Bob, what ever that woman wants or needs, she gets as far as I'm concerned. If anyone ever says no to that woman, it's going to be you Mr. Hightower, not me.! Without any more talking the four men ate their lunch consisting of an exceptionally good bowl of beef stew, some fried cornbread, and a big glass of ice cold buttermilk. For dessert they had a big slice of applesauce cake. Hightower had no idea that Rachel could bake, he knew that she could cook, but baking is a different thing. Then Dorothy came out of the bedroom telling Rachel that she had put the babies down for a map and then she turned and asked the four men, "I hope you like the applesauce cake, it took me two tries to get it right, but I think it will pass muster."

Rachel turned around with a smile on her face and said, "now, gentlemen, I never told you that I fixed the cake. All I said is that I made the beef stew. My sister was always the one who wanted to learn to bake, me, I have a hard enough time just making biscuits. Then with a girlish giggle she turned back to the stove and dipped her and Dorothy up a bowl of beef stew and then the two ladies joined the four men in conversation and laughter! After having a very hearty lunch. Andrews, Lewis, and Mason returned to their security post, and Hightower and Rachel and Dorothy settled down in the living room to just spend some time together and make plans for tomorrow. They sat and talked about the judge and Amy and the funny things they used to do. They even talked about when they argued it was always comical and they both ended up laughing, simply because what they argued about meant nothing at all. It was a plain fact that the two of them loved each other very much and no matter what happened, no matter what obstacle or situation come their way they stood side-by-side and took it on together. Rachel was doing what Hightower hoped she would do, she was remembering all of the good times that she and Dorothy shared with their mom and dad. Both of the girls were taking on some of Amy's ways, such as her sense of humor, but also the times when she could be very Stern. In short, when Amy layed down the law, even the judge did not argue with her.

Dorothy disappeared for just a few minutes and when she came back she had to photo albums and a separate box full of newspaper articles and write ups about the judge, and there was write ups about the work that Amy had done helping people who had lost their homes due to wild fires or in the earner days Indian attacks and quite a few of them had lost their land and homes to carpetbaggers after the Civil War. The judge had been instrumental in stopping these people from coming into Texas, and stealing land and herds of cattle. He made an example of one man who thought he was above the law because he has a brother who a senator in Tennessee. The man was found guilty of murder and the judge hung him the very next day. This sent a message that their carpet bagging days were over and legal theft would not be tolerated. Every Sheriff of every little town was made aware of the judge's ruling and it was plain that if they allowed it to happen in their jurisdiction they would be held accountable the same as the men who had done the dirty deed. So needless to say, these Sheriff's quickly learned that no amount of money was worth going against judge Walter Tatum. It's not to say a few didn't try, but the people of their community put a stop to it, and they done it by forcibly throwing him out of office and then running him out of town. Most of the time the deputies were allowed to stay, but they were giving a choice abide by the ruling of judge Tatum, or gather up their things and get out of town.

The girls were very proud of their father for the way he stood up for the people of Texas, and for the people of southwestern Louisiana, against the land grabbers and political crooks. Many people from the North came down South and tried to run for office, some even tried to buy their way into politics, and then there were a few who tried to use threats, intimidation and even murder to get into office, but that too, didn't work Rachel turned to Hightower and said, "Edward, do you realize that you're getting just about the same reputation as my father had. You wearing that badge with honor and dignity, and you make it a point to administer the law fairly, rich or poor doesn't matter to you, right and wrong does. You told me and Dorothy a while ago that our parents were very proud of us, well, Mr. Hightower, I for one am very proud of you and I always will be." Dorothy spoke up and said, "everything she said. Edward, I agree with as long as you are alive, my father will never die, simply because you are a lot like him and I know that he was proud to be able to call you his friend, the same as he did your father." "What say we change the subject. Dorothy when are you and Mason going to get hitched?" "Whenever he gets up the nerve to ask me, which is, I hope, before I become an old maid." "I was thinking Dorothy that when and if he does ask you, I was thinking that we should build you and Mason your own house. I would say not more than 100 feet from this house in whatever direction you to go. So I suggest that you do a little prodding to get Mason in gear. This ranch would no longer exist. If it hadn't been for your father, so as far as I'm concerned this ranch belongs to Rachel and you, me, I just live here." "I wished you people would stop talking like I'm not here. I'm sitting right here in this room. The way that Dorothy has been shying away from me. I wasn't too sure that she was still interested, and the one thing I have learned about this family is you do not push them or try to get them in a corner to get your way about something. No, Sir, I am not getting on the wrong side of these two Tatum women." "How about me, do you have any qualms about getting on my bad side, Hightower ask?" Mason looked up and smiled and said, "not really, all you would do is shoot me, these two women would probably grab a frying pan a piece and beat me to death."

Hightower scratched his head, studied for just a minute and then said, "I never thought of it like that Mason, but it seems to me that you just might be right, after all those two Tatum women are pretty rowdy." Hightower immediately received a slap on his shoulder from Rachel and she said, "I'm beginning to feel like Mason, stop talking about me, I'm sitting right here and if you need something to assure yourself that I am setting right here, I can accommodate you." While she was saying this, Rachel reached back on top of the heating stove and picked up a small pan that was usually full of water, Thinking that it was time for a retreat. Hightower threw up both of his hands and said, "you don't have to get my attention ma'am, I'm already married, and said, "just as long as you remember who butter's your bread, and whose's the boss of his loony bin we'll get along just fine." That little statement brought forth a resounding round of laughter from everyone.

For the rest of the afternoon, with the exception of a few people stopping by to see how they were getting along, the time was spent talking about the present, remembering the past, and of course planning for the future. Not only for Dorothy and Mason, but for Hightower Junior, and Rebecca Marie. The one thing Hightower requested from Rachel, is that if anything happened to him. She would not let Junior become a law man.

Rachel was quick to respond to that, she made it plain that she would not stand in his way of becoming a law man because his father stood for law and order, right and wrong. She couldn't see that following in his father's footsteps could in any way be considered a bad path to take. Then she said, "but we don't have to worry about that for another 18 or 20 years."! Dorothy stood up and said, "I need to go for a walk, is that all right Edward,?" "Only if you take an armed escort with you, Mason would you escort the lady on an evening walk, remember now, she's your responsibility keep her safe."!!!

After they had gone out the front door, Rachel turned to Hightower and ask, "do you think that he will ask her soon,? Or is she going to have to trap him?" "She won't have to trap him Rachel, she's already got him hooked, she just has to reel him in. I think the idea about building them a house is a good idea. I would like to have it close enough that we can both use the same well what do you think about having the house built close enough to together that there can be a fenced in yard, so when the babies start walking they can go outside and play. Eventually I know that there's going to be more than two children out there, I'm hoping that Dorothy will get busy and have at least three of her own. As soon as I stop breast-feeling the twins Edward I want another child another girl and I want her named Amy Rose. Do you think it would be all right to name her that?" Looking at Rachel and nodding his head, Hightower said, "absolutely"!!!

Chapter 5

The afternoon passed very quickly and the atmosphere in the house was subdued, but not in a bad way. The house was quiet while the twins slept so Rachel told Andrew, Lewis, and Mason to go upstairs and they will find a bedroom that has three single beds in it, and she ordered them to lie down and get them a good nights sleep and she would wake them in the morning in time to get ready to ride into town. She handed each man his washed and ironed uniform and said, as if they were her children, "now you make sure to hang these up, don't just throw them down. Some time between tonight and tomorrow morning. Please if you will gentlemen shine your boots. If any of you think you need a haircut come and see Dorothy. She always raved about how good she cutting hair. She cut dads all the time and she has always been really good with was with a pair of scissors and a comb. There were times when Dorothy even shaved our father, but only when mom was too busy to shave him."

Andrews looked over at Hightower and ask, "are you sure there's nothing else I can do to make things any easier on you boss?" "You can call me Mr. Hightower, or Edward, you can call me a dirty son of a bitch, but don't ever call me boss again. You've got your orders Cpl. now I suggest that you and your two comrades carry them out to the letter."

"I meant no disrespect, it just doesn't seem right to be calling you as if we don't know each other, or that we just met. If it's all right with you, I'd just as soon call you Edward, Ed just doesn't seem right, and Mt. Hightower has the feeling of being old, and hell, I'm older than you are."

Andrews turned to walk away Hightower said, "Cpl., I apologize for being so blunt, you are right, we have known each other a long time and we have rode through some hard trails together. We have even fought side-by-side anything that you think is appropriate even if it's boss, just as long as you don't treat me like your boss. When we ride together like we did the last time in New Mexico. I consider us to be a team, the four of us and I think we make one damn good team. Now go get you some sleep. Cpl. you've earned it."

Andrews had left and went upstairs, Hightower turned to Rachel and kind of dropped his head and said, "I guess tomorrow is getting to me, just a little bit, maybe I need to get me about three fingers of whiskey and go out and set on the front porch for a little while. I might even think back to how my father used to speak about your father, and just how good of friends they were. I know the first time I met your dad I was just a little bit queasy in the stomach because of all the stories my dad had told me about the judge Walter Tatum. How he had struck the fear of God into the hearts of a lot of people who were regularly getting into trouble. Then he told me the stories about the carpetbaggers that came after the war, and how your dad single-handedly declared war on them. I'll bet you didn't know Rachel that they actually tried to have your father killed, and my dad said, instead of running or taking cover your dad picked up a Winchester and my dad and your dad walked into the person's office that had put a bounty on the judge's head , arrested him, taking everything he had accumulated in his short stay in Lake Charles and to the best of my recollection about what my father said. Your dad laid the barrel of that Winchester on the chest of the man and ask him if he still wanted to kill him? When the man said no. Then your father told him there was a stage leaving this town going West in about two hours, and he had best be on that stage, or else he was likely to end up in a pine box."

"That was back, just after the war had ended, Dorothy, and I were only about 10 or 12 years old at the time and we remember how angry Mama got at him for picking up that rifle and putting his life on the line to enforce the law. Looking back now I understand why he did it, and more over, Edward, understand why you put your life on the line every time you put that badge on and if anybody should be proud of anybody. It is, I who should be the proudest of you. I must admit Edward, I was taken by you the very first day I ever laid eyes on you. I wanted to believe that some way, somehow you would be a major part of my life. God has smiled on me, I feel that he put you here because he knew soon he was going to take mom and dad and he felt Dorothy and I needed someone to love and project us, that's you. Edward, you are my knight in shining armor and I love you more every day." Then she put her hands on each side of Hightower's face as she kissed him, not once not twice, but three times and said, "it's time for the babies final feeding for the night, I need to change them and feed them, maybe they will sleep through the night. I just hope the sun is shining tomorrow."

As Rachel retired into the bedroom, Hightower stepped out onto the porch, but not before stopping and getting him a glass full to the brim of Kentucky bourbon. For some reason or another, the longer this day went on the more at ease, Hightower got. He now knew that the Indians had as much of a grudge against Elizabeth Carter and her gang As he did, and he had three other men that would stick with him through thick and thin, and have his back, always. It was time for the killing spree of Elizabeth Carter to end. There would be no sending Elizabeth to prison, there would be no bullet in her, she was going to hang. He knew that it wasn't the Christian way to feel, but he just couldn't seem to get past all of the pain and misery that she had caused for a little over 2 ½ years. She must pay for the murder of her husband, whose last name was Kershaw. The murder of the two deputies who were escorting her to prison. The murder of the high Sheriff of Las Cruses. And last but not least the cold-blooded murder of Walter, and Amy Tatum. There were undoubtedly other murders that they didn't know about, but they did know about nine bank robberies. Making a promise to himself, Hightower said, "this time she will not escape, she will not elude the law, this I promise to myself.

Then taking a good swallower out of the glass. He leaned back in his chair and studied the sky. It looked as if the clouds were breaking up, because every once in a while he would see a star. Then a breeze started blowing and the clouds started moving a little faster and suddenly the moon in all of its glory shined through the clouds. It was as if God himself had granted Rachel the promise of a cloud free day.

Unaware to Hightower, the top Sgt. had been sitting in the shadows on the other end of the porch and he brought Hightower back to reality when he ask, "are you having trouble sleeping Sir? If you are, you've got a good remedy in your hand." Turning to the top Sgt. Hightower said, "I'd offer you slug, but you're on guard duty top, maybe tomorrow morning before the funeral we can share one in a toast to the judge and Amy." "I got no problem with that Mr. Hightower, no problem at all. Then the top Sgt. settled back in his chair, in the shadows with that Winchester laid up against one leg and a shotgun laid up against the other and a 45 in his hand. Hightower could tell by the look on the man's face that he was deadly serious about protecting this family. To a lot of soldiers to draw duty like this to protect a man's family was an honor and you could see the pride in his face, because she had been chosen to lead all of these troopers in protecting the women and the children that made up the Hightower family.!!

Hightower set out the porch for quite a while, as a matter of fact they had changed guard twice and it suddenly dawned on him that it had to be well after midnight and he needed to get him some sleep so reluctantly, he downed the rest of his whiskey and took off his boots. Left his work boots on the front porch, so he wouldn't make any noise going into the house and try to make it into the bed without disturbing everybody, looking up at the night sky, he said "thank you for this day Lord, and I pray you grant me one more at least. I pray you watch over my family and these brave troopers. Now on a more personal note Lord, I ask that you allow me to catch this evil woman and put this whole dirty business behind us, it's time the killing stopped." Then he stood up and started through the door into the house, he suddenly stopped and turned, looked back up at the sky and said, "sorry Lord, I almost forgot, Amen."

As Hightower stepped into the bedroom he made his way over to the two cribs and looked down at the faces of his children and once again, he thanked God for giving him back something that he had missed for so many years, the gentleness of having a woman sharing your life and to have given him roots by allowing him to form a family. Very quietly and very gently Hightower ease himself into the bed beside Rachel. As he lay there in the bed thinking about tomorrow and everything that would be going on during the day he realized that he was a very lucky man. He had what every man on the frontier yearns for, a wife, his children, and a ranch that is paid for lock stock and barrel. And extended family, and friends who ask no questions, but have his back, no matter what.

Hightower closed his eyes with the intention of his memories turning into dreams, and his dreams transporting him to piece and tranquility when the sun rose the next morning there wasn't a cloud in the sky. The moment the sun peaked over the horizon you could feel its warmth it was as if someone was telling Rachel that her wish had been granted. There was a good breeze blowing, which was helping get rid of some of the standing water that was all over the yard, the compound, and the stockade. Setting up on the edge of the bed Hightower could hear voices in the kitchen, so slipping his work jeans and shirt back on, and then for the first time since Rachel had bought them he put on his house slippers and he was surprised at just how good they felt on his feet still, they weren't boots. When he entered the kitchen, he noticed Mason had assumed his post, so he turned around stopping in the dining room and seen Lewis sitting at his post, so he said, "come on it's time for some coffee and I do believe there's breakfast also a brewing." when he entered the kitchen he was met by Rachel and Dorothy and they said at the same time, "good morning."

Before Hightower could get set down there was a cup of coffee waiting on him, and he wondered why Rachel and Dorothy was in such a good mood. He became extremely suspicious. When he seen Rachel placed a towel over something setting on the counter, but he decided if whatever it was on the counter was taking Rachel and Dorothy's minds off of the funeral today, Then he would just let it go.

"Sis, and I thought we should get an early start this morning, I hope you don't mind Edward, but I wanted, or should I say Dorothy and I wanted to have a few moments alone with mom and dad before the funeral starts. Mrs. Bitterman who lives on that small farm just down the road is coming by to take care of the twins. I just don't think that going to a funeral at their age is the right thing to do, besides miss Bitterman and the twins get along quite well. She has babysit for us a few times when you were in New Mexico, so that we could go into town and do some shopping. She is engaged to a young man that works as a court officer in the courthouse."

"I do believe I met that young man, I think he was the one that I met the first day that I came in to Lake Charles looking for your father, if it is the same young man, I think maybe I owe him an apology for giving him such a hard time that day."

Then, Hightower preceded to tell the story of how the young man had tried to take Hightower's weapon and how Hightower had forced him to take him before the judge and force the judge to instruct the young man to take his weapon, and then the judge all prepared to do that until he had told the judge, his name and then the judge all but through the young man out of his office and for the rest of the day the judge and Hightower spent talking and reliving old times with his father. That was the day that he met Amy and she took that arrowhead out of his right shoulder and it was the first day that he had met Rachel. It reminded him of the 10 days that he had spent being cared for by Rachel and Amy and Dorothy, it also reminded him of the friendship that had blossomed between the judge and him. Suddenly Hightower sadness come over him as he thought of that friendship and he remembered something his father had told him, "son through your life, you will meet some people who make a great impression on your life, you will meet some people that instantly you admire, you will meet people that instantly will take to you, and these people will offer you the greatest gift that you will ever receive, it's the gift of boundless friendship. That's the kind of friendship that will gladly step in between you and harms way. There will be people that you feel the same way about, people who you would gladly lay down your life for to protect them. If through your entire life. You can count on one hand the people who fit into this category, then my son, you will be a very rich man because in your lifetime you will have many friends, but the close friends, you'll be able to count on one hand, and those are ones that make life worthwhile. Even when they are not around you, they will be with you always."

Suddenly everything seemed to just swell up inside of Hightower and for the very first time in his life, he cried. oh he had shed tears before, but he had never cried, excusing himself from the kitchen table. Hightower went back into the bedroom. It was hard for Hightower to let anyone see him breakdown this way he didn't feel ashamed about crying, but he did feel ashamed of allowing that weakness to show. Just as he had set down on the edge of the bed. He became aware that Rachel was standing directly in front of him and then she walked up close to him and put her arms around him without saying a word she held him close and let him cry.

After a few minutes, Hightower was able to get a hold of himself and he set up straight and looked up into Rachel's eyes and he said, "I am so sorry that you seen this." "Well, I'm not. I always felt that there was more to you Edward, in my heart I always knew that you had a soft spot, and that someday something would happen that would cause that soft spot to surface. I know how close you and father had become, we all could see it, everyone could see it. except you. There is nothing in this world wrong with crying for a friend, it just shows that you care."

Then Rachel stepped back, taking him by hand she led him back into the kitchen and it was as though nothing had happened at all. Andrews, Lewis, and Mason, along with Dorothy never stopped their conversation. Rachel looked up just for an instant and said, "Edward, you had best eat your breakfast before it gets cold." Hightower remembered that his father always said, "showing your feelings to your family is never a bad thing."

After breakfast was over, Hightower went to be bedroom to change his clothes, while Rachel and Dorothy cleaned up the breakfast dishes. He was setting on the edge of the bed putting some polish on his boots and brushing them off when Rachel came into the bedroom and brushing up to Hightower and said, "unzip me please." Then she preceded to set down at a little desk and brush her hair out. Then she preceded to set down what she needed on her face, which was mostly just a face powder and a little blush, then she walked over and slipped into a neatly ironed black dress and then she walked over to Hightower and turned around once again, and said, "zip me up, please. She already had black stockings on, so all she had left to do was to put her shoes on and she was ready to go.

Slipping his boots on Hightower stood up and he heard Rachel laugh, then she said, "one of these days. Edward, I am going to teach you how to tie a string tie." She then walked up to him and preceded to tie his tie the way she thought it should be done. When she had finished. He looked in the mirror and decided that she was right, it did look better.

As they walked out of the bedroom Dorothy was seated in the living room talking to a young lady, which Hightower assumed was miss Bitterman. Immediately Dorothy introduced Hightower to the young lady and Dorothy said, "the general has appointed four men to stand guard in this house and the remaining eight men are to stay outside. There will be other troopers on guard at the stockade, so there is no reason to worry about the house or the children, or miss Bitterman." Then Dorothy preceded to show miss Bitterman where all of the diapers and baby powder and other stuff was, and that there was food on the stove for her and there was also one bottle a piece for the babies, because Rachel had decided it was time for the babies to start nursing a bottle and not her.

While miss Bitterman was being shown around the house and where everything was. Hightower had gone out to harness up the buckboard and while he was doing that Andrews, Lewis, and Mason, where saddling their horses. Hightower had to admit that they looked pretty snazzy in their freshly washed and ironed uniforms and they were doing their best not to get any dirt or cause any wrinkles in their uniforms and that's hard to do when trying to saddle a spirited animal.

As Hightower was hooking up the two horses to the buckboard he seen something lying underneath the seat, so curiosity got the best of him and he walked up and reached under the seat and pulled out a small silver flask the enscription on the flask read, "to judge Walter Tatum, thanks from the city of Lake Charles." Placing it is his coat pocket, he climbed abroad the buckboard and drove it back up to the front porch. One of the troopers who was standing his post step down and took hold of the bridal of the closest horse, saluting and said I'll hold onto them for you Sir." Hightower thanked him and started up onto the porch. He never made it inside of the house, because Rachel and Dorothy were on their way out. Dorothy being the tomboy that she was jumped up on the buckboard and seated before Rachel even started to get into the buckboard so Hightower just reached and took Rachel with both hands around her waist and sat her on the seat Rachel smiled and with that girlish giggle that he was so accustomed to. She said, "see, I told you that I was back to my normal weight, so don't you ever tell me that I am plump and sassy again." Hightower just smiled saying, "yes, dear." And climbed aboard taking the reins he turned the team toward town.

All the way to town. Rachel and Dorothy spent their time looking at the scenery and talking about each place that their mom and dad had taken them for a picnic, or for a Berry picking spree, or even to take a dip in their favorite swimming hole. They brought up memories of thing that they had done together as a family. They even talked about the time that the four of them spent the entire afternoon feeding a bunch of squirrels, they remembered before the day was over. They had the squirrels literally eating out of their hands, and for some reason those squirrels were never afraid. And then there was the grouchy old groundhog that was so accustomed to seeing their dad that he would come out of his hole and fuss at the judge, the judge would laugh and then make the same sound back to the groundhog, and evidently it would make the groundhog mad because he would really throw a fit it was as if another groundhog had invaled his territory. Walter just called him "old man."

As they pulled into town, Hightower had never seen so many people in their Sunday go to meeting clothes in his life. Even the shopkeepers and the barber with the exception of having their coats on were dressed as if they were going to church. It appeared that the whole town was going to give the judge and Amy a very fitting sendoff. As they pulled up in front of the funeral parlor. The proprietor came out onto the boardwalk and said, "the Lord has made a beautiful day for the judge and Amy to come home and be with him."

Rachel said, "my sister and I would like a few minutes with our mom and dad alone, if it's all right with you?" "Absolutely, you two ladies take as much time as you need, there isn't anybody here in a big hurry,"

Hightower got down from the buggy and first helped Rachel down, then he helped Dorothy down. Looking at Rachel Hightower said, "you and Dorothy go ahead and pay your respects, take as much time as you want, I'll wait for you out here." Then he reached into his inside coat pocket and brought out the flask and handed it to Rachel and said , "I found it this morning in the buckboard, I didn't know if you would want to keep it or let him take it with him."

Rachel took the flask looked at it, shook it and then said, "the Lord will tolerate a glass of wine, but he would never tolerate hard liquor, and with that she opened up the top of the flask and handed it to Hightower and said, "kill it, if you please." Hightower turned the flask up and into swallows the Kentucky Bourbon was gone. Reaching up and taking the flask back. Rachel replaced the top and carrying it in her hand she disappeared into the funeral parlor.

Andrews had gotten down from his horse and walked up to Hightower and said, "been walking too much, settin on a horse ain't as comfortable as it used to be, it must be that or my saddles gone bad." Knowing full well that only way a saddle can be damaged is to be extremely water soaked Hightower said," it ain't the saddle is gone bad, you just lost that padding that you've been carrying around for so many years and replaced it with muscle from walking." While still rubbing his bottom Andrews smiled and said, "ain't it's so." Looking up at Lewis and Mason Hightower said, "you two might as well get down and get some circulation in your legs too, we could be here quite a while, or just a couple of minutes."

From what Hightower had learned there was going to be a grave side service and the Rev. that used to play checkers with the judge on the courthouse steps was going to perform the service. Remembering what the judge said about the Rev. Hightower giggle to himself. The judge used to say, "the only way I can beat that old preacher in checkers, is get him drunk. "Then he would add, "it usually cost me about two dollars every afternoon that we played for whiskey, the old preacher can drank more than I can and still walk away without staggering." They both had been young men when they had first moved to Lake Charles. As a matter of fact, they both arrived on the same wagon train. Then, Hightower realized that he had no idea how old the judge or Amy was. Turning to the proprietor Hightower ask if he knew how old the judge was, the elderly undertaker replied, "according to the records in the courthouse. The judge was born March 31, 1836, miss Amy was born November 2, 1838." Then as he turned to go back in to the parlor, Hightower heard him say, August 14, 1883 is day that Lake Charles will always remember."

Doing some figuring in his head. Hightower figured out that the judge was only 47 years old, Amy was 45. Andrews making the same calculations shook his head, and said, "that's just too damn young to die." Then he walked over to his horse opened his saddle bag and took out a pint of whiskey and without waiting he took a good stiff drink and handed it to Lewis, who in turn handed it to Mason,who in turn handed it to Andrews. Turning to face Hightower, he handed him the bottle and Hightower, smiled and said, "no thanks. I've already had mine. And before they come out of the parlor. I suggest you hide that or my wife just might have your hide." Andrews looked at the bottle which only had a bout one good swig left in it, and said, "no sense in letting it go to waste." And with no hesitation at all, he downed it.

Rachel and Dorothy was in the funeral parlor for a little more than 30 minutes, and when they came out, both of the girls seem to have a lot better hold on things than they did before they went in. Since Hightower didn't go inside with the girls he had no idea what went on, except that a gentleman walked out of the funeral parlor before Rachel and Dorothy could get in the buckboard. When he walked out Rachel looked at him and said, "thanks for the understanding and I'll do my best to try and remember what you said then without introducing Hightower, she said, "let's go Edward, I wouldn't want to be late or have any people sitting and waiting for us to get there.

As Hightower climbed onto the buckboard, the young man followed Rachel and Dorothy out of the funeral parlor walked up and stuck out his hand and said, "I'm sorry Mr. Hightower for no introducing myself sooner, I am Tim Blankenship, and I'm the pastor of the new Baptist Church just East of town on the main trail. I knew your father-in-law we visited quite often in the courthouse, simply because on Sunday it was my job to hold services for anyone that was incarcerated in the judge's jail. I hope you don't mind, Sir, but I will be attending the funeral and I will be more than glad to help in any way I can. I really liked judge Tatum and his wife, they were like a second set of parents to me. The judge always had time to talk or discuss something. He often encouraged me by saying, "my God man, if you have a question about something, don't walk around with that question in your mind, open your mouth and ask somebody who just might know the answer." Many is the time that the judge would put aside what he was doing and talk to me and explained to me how in some ways the laws of man are a lot like the laws of God. He would say, "why wouldn't the two sets of laws be similar, man lives by the laws of God, but he is governed by the laws of man." I always found that a very profane statement. I won't hold you up any longer, Mr. Hightower, God bless you and your family in your time of grief and may God ride with you always."

Hightower set there holding the reins in his hand for a couple of minutes watching the young pastor walk away down the boardwalk with this Bible tucked under his arm, his head held high and a bit of a swagger in his walk. Not knowing if Rachel was listening or not, but Hightower mumbled to himself, "someday that young man will make his mark and it will last for a long time."

Hightower started the two ponies off at an easy walk and decided they would keep that gate all the way to the graveyard. They passed directly by the courthouse and Hightower halted the ponies and said to Rachel, "right there on those steps is where my life changed." Continuing on down the street nobody in the buckboard had spoken a word since the courthouse, and no one spoke. When they pulled up to the gates of the graveyard. Hightower got down and using a lead rope tied the two ponies to a hitching post, and then he returned to the buckboard and helped Rachel down and then Dorothy.

Rachel reached and took Hightower's arm and Hightower noticed that Dorothy reached and took Mason's arm and then they preceded to the plot that the judge had bought years ago. There was one large headstone and all it had on it was in large letters, "the Tatum family." Then there was a list of names. Hightower got one hell of a surprise when the funeral wagon opened his back door. There was no coffins. Unbeknown to Hightower, the judge and Amy had planned to be cremated so that every member of their family could rest together under this one stone. I didn't have the heart to tell you Edward, that there would be no need for pallbearers. Rachel said" "I wished you had of told me sooner then I could've saved everyone a whole lot of preparation." Andrews stepped up beside Hightower's and said, "the other day when we brought the judge and Amy into town. I made the remark that we were going to be pallbearers and the undertaker told me that was a nice gesture, but there would be no coffins only urns, then he informed the that the judge and Amy were going to be cremated. It was there wish, so you see Edward, you were the only one who didn't know. We kind of figured the three of us could still escort them, we just wouldn't be carried anything. Your wife and Dorothy will carry the two urns and I kind of figured we would escort them. I was ordered by your wife not to tell you. Sorry, that's one request that I couldn't deny."

"You're doing what your father wanted, that's all that matters Rachel." As they walked arm in arm up to the funeral wagon Rachel and Dorothy took their arms back and preceded alone each daughter was handed a very beautiful urn, holding it cradled in their hands and leaning against their chest. The walked, escorted by three decked out troopers, and one spit and polished United States marshal. Holes had been dug side-by-side at the base of the headstone. The holes were big enough to hold the urns and were the full six-foot deep.

Two small carriages just big enough for one urn in each one sat on the ground beside each hole. Rachel placed the judge's urn on the small wooden platform and stepped back. Dorothy done the same wit here mother and then she stepped back. Also then the two locked arms and stood that way. While the funeral director picked up one urn and lowered the small carriage down into the hole and then dropped the rope into the hole also. Then he repeated the process with Amy. He then turned around and said something very quietly to the two girls and then as he turned around and walked away. The preacher stepped up and said something in Latin and then clutching his Bible to his chest. He spoke in English saying, "these two beautiful soul were great believers in life, and harmony, and love. They practiced each one of these every day, and they practiced it on each other. Their biggest believe was in God and the hereafter. The judge asked me to make that statement that I started with in Latin, simply because he liked to speak the language. What I said was, "I ask you, God of gods, lord of lords to accept these two souls into thy bosom."

Then the old preacher stepped back and dropped his head, kneeling down. He made the sign of the cross and as if rehearsed everyone in attendance done the same. There was not a sound to be heard except sound of the preacher's voice as he quoted the Lord's prayer. As Hightower looked from face to face, 90% of the people had tears on their cheeks. Almost as if on cue, a large red bird landed on top of the headstone, seemingly unafraid. It looked around chirped a couple of times and flew away. Everyone else had their heads bowed, except Hightower and it seemed he had been the only one to see the bird and he thought to himself. "Maybe the bird was sent here to escort Walter and Amy on their final trip." Hightower felt a slight smile come to his face and he also noticed that a tear had welled up in his eyes, but had not yet rolled down his cheeks, but this time he didn't wipe them off before they fell, this time he'd just let them fall.

Chapter 6

Rachel and Dorothy after the services was over, pulled the undertaker and the preacher aside and had a quick conversation that lasted no more than a couple of minutes. This made Hightower think that there was something going on, but he figured Rachel would tell him sooner or later, so he'd just let things slide. When they came back to the buckboard the undertaker and the preacher escorted them, and the last thing the preacher said to the two girls was, "I'll be out to the ranch, either late this evening, or first thing in the morning, it that's okay."

Rachel just shook her head yes and said, "whenever you can will be from fine with us." All the way back to the ranch. There was very few words that were spoken. All, Rachel said was, "if you don't mind Edward, just let the ponies walk, I feel like watching nature for a little while."

Dorothy was setting on the back of the buckboard with Mason at her side. Andrews and Lewis were bringing up of the rear and leading Mason's horse. Dorothy kept talking to Mason, but her voice was so low that Hightower could not hear a single word she was saying, and all Mason was doing was shaking his head yes.

It took a little over an hour to make it back to the ranch, but Hightower didn't mind it was a nice little drive on a very beautiful day and he was getting to spend some quality time with his wife. When they drove up to the front porch, miss Bitterman had the twins out on the porch on a blanket playing with them, and there was four troopers standing guard, on and around the porch. Miss Bitterman stood up as they came to a stop in front of the porch. Rachel ask her if the kids had been behaveing theirselves, she just smiled and said they were perfect angels. Dorothy had already gotten off the buckboard and walk up on the front porch and sat down with the twins, while Hightower helped Rachel off the buckboard and then said, "I'm going to take the buckboard down to the barn and unhitched the ponies then turn them into the pasture after I brush them down real good." As he led the ponies off. Rachel hollered at him and said, "don't be too long Edward, I've got something I need to talk to you about." Hightower just looked back at Rachel and shook his head yes and then continued walking.

It only took Hightower about 20 minutes to unharnessed the ponies and rub them down and on his way back to the house, he was met by the old trooper and he asked, "are you okay son, funerals always did drain all of my energy, especially when it's the funeral of someone that you care a lot about. If some time you'd like to talk, it's been said that I'm a pretty good listener." "When you get off duty old timer, I just might get a bottle and a couple of glasses and take you up on that, if you can listen and drink at the same time?"

The old timer smiled real big and rubbed his whiskered chin and said, "I listen real good. When I got a glass of whiskey in my hand, you'd be surprised at just how smart I get after three or four fingers of whiskey." "I don't doubt that the least bit, I've known a lot of people who got real smart after drinking whiskey, but unfortunately very few of the could remember what they talked about." The old timer laughed and said, "Yep, I've been in that situation a few times myself."

As he left the old timer and started back toward the ranch hose, he wondered what it was that Rachel want to talk to him about. He had a gut feeling that there was a little bit of mischief in the wind, but he just couldn't put his finger on it, anyway. He would soon find out because Rachel and Dorothy were sitting alone with the babies and the front porch. They seem to be having a very serious conversation about something, "I think you had better sit down Edward, this is not going to take very long, but it's going to come as a shock." Dorothy handed him a glass of whiskey and said, "bottoms up."

Rachel and Dorothy looked at each other and finally, Dorothy said, "no sense to put it off Rachel, get it said." Rachel looked up at Hightower and said, "you always said that the easiest way to say something was to just say it, so here goes. Edward those urns that we buried today were empty. Dad did not want to be buried in the ground and neither did mom. But the townsfolk wanted that stone as a symbol of how much they honored my dad and mom for their dedication to this community. So quite a few years ago, dad and mom set us down and told us the plans that they had made. As far as the town folks know mom and dad is buried in the graveyard right in under their names on that stone, but in reality they will be delivered here either this evening or tomorrow morning. By the funeral director and the young preacher that you met yesterday. Only the undertaker, the preacher, and Dorothy and I knew about this. Originally they were to be put on the mantle over the fireplace in the house in town, but you came into the story and their place of residence changed from town to here. Dorothy and I discussed the fact that we need to let you in on our little secret, but you had so much on your mind concerning Elizabeth Carter, that we decided to wait until the very last minute. We just didn't think it would come so soon. Mom and dad expected to live at least to 60, 65 years old, they never once thought that Elizabeth Carter and her gang would cut them down while they were seated on the front porch. I'm sorry that we deceived you, please forgive me for not telling you sooner but I was only trying to honor my parents last wish."

"Rachel, you must have a pretty low opinion of me, I could never be mad at you for trying to do what's right and for trying to honor your parents, but I can be a little bit upset that you and your sister didn't trust me enough to tell me about this. But then again I can't stay angry, disappointed, maybe for a little while, but I'll get over it." Then Hightower stood up and looked around and with a questioning look on his face he ask, "where is miss Bitterman, we need to be getting her home. I'm quite sure she got things at her house that she needs to be doing."?

Dorothy spoke up and said, "oh, you don't have to worry about miss Bitterman, Andrew is escorting her back to her little farm. By the way, Edward I'm surprised you didn't know that Andrew and miss Bitterman had been seeing each other ever since the day the troops arrived here. I'm surprised you didn't know that Andrew was raised on the same little farm that miss Bitterman now lives on, so when he came back to settle his parents affairs he sold the ranch to miss Bitterman's mother and father."

Hightower leaned back in his chair and started to remove his hat realized that he wasn't wearing one, so he scratched his head anyway, and with a cockeyed smile on his face he said, "it seems that there is a lot of things that's been going on around here that I don't know anything about, so I guess we should all set down with a little bit of whiskey, or coffee, or some tea. And start telling some of the secrets that I should know about. Here I am about to go after a cold-blooded killer, and I am going to have three men backing me up, but what I didn't know is that two of the three will have their minds on a woman instead of watching my back. Now, don't you think that I should of known about this a long time ago? As it stands right now. I'll probably have to find three other men to back me up." Just as Hightower started to say something else. There was a voice that came from behind him, and it said very plainly, "no, Sir, you don't have to look for anybody, the three of us have a score to settle just as much as you do so, Mr. Hightower, you don't have to worry about Andrew, Mason, or me. We'll be there whenever we're needed, and that is a fact, Sir,"

Recognizing the voice Hightower turned around and from the look on Lewis's face, the young trooper was ready to fight, and from the way he was standing. He didn't much care who it was. "You ask the general if we could ride with you and we said yes, and we meant it then and the three of us still mean it, but if you've changed your mind. We can't do anything about that, but we firmly intend to keep our word."!!!..........

After speaking his mind, Lewis snapped to attention, saluted. Done a snappy about-face and walked off. Hightower had offended the young trooper and he regretted that the way down to his bones.

As Hightower set there watching Lewis walk away. There was movement in the yard that caught his eye. There was two cotton tails that were feeding on the grass and they had stopped feeding and were looking in Hightower's direction. Standing on their hind legs as if they had an opinion about what Hightower's direction should be on their hind legs as if they had an opinion about what Hightower had said also. Hightower looked at the two rabbits and said, "any other time I'd already have you in a pot, but today is your lucky day, today I eat crow."

Turning back to Rachel Hightower said, "I must apologize for anything that I said that evidently has upset not only Lewis, but you and Dorothy. You must understand to them. I have been in Indian wars. I have hunted down outlaws, and I've found myself, before going into a gunfight, thinking about Rachael, and about the twins. Wondering what will happen to them if I fall today. Rachel and I are married and I know, that you worry about me whenever I leave this house. Therefore, I am quite sure that Mason worries about you, Dorothy. Just the same as Andrew will think and worry about miss Bitterman. I don't want it on my conscience that I could possibly be the reason why one or possibly even both of these young men never know the serenity and warmth of having a woman to cuddle to, or to just spend time talking too."

"You need to have more faith in these three men, after all. Edward, they are trained soldiers, they have also fought Indians, and thanks to you, they have also chased down outlaws, and again, thanks to you, they have survived gunfights. So my advice to you, Mr. Hightower, is don't under estimate these men, they are dedicated and loyal to their beliefs and they take their duty very Seriously." After making this statement, Dorothy got up from her chair, tossed her hair back and disappeared into the house.

"You were wrong to question the integrity of those three men Edward, and before it goes any further, you need to make it right. You need to apologize to all three of those men, and you need to do it now.!"

Hightower looked at Rachel and said, "you're right, I'll take care of it right now." Hightower got up out of his chair and stepped off of the front porch never looking back and as soon as his feet touched the ground. He hollered at Lewis and ask him to wait just a minute. Lewis stopped and waited for him. When Hightower got within speaking range to Lewis, he told him to go find Mason, and Andrews and meet him in the barn as soon as possible. While Lewis went looking to find Mason Hightower headed for the general's office.

Walking in to the general's office Hightower took off his hat and pitched it over on a little table, then he walked over to the general's desk and set down in a chair. Without waiting for the general to say anything,

Hightower said, "I'm not going to take Andrews or Mason with me in search Elizabeth Carter. I will take Lewis, so I need two more men general. I need two men that's got experience, that are excellent shots, and have no problem in taking orders. And most of all are not tied up in a romance. Do you have a couple of men that sounds like?"

"What got into you, Hightower? I thought Andrews, Lewis, and Mason were going to be your backup?" Andrews has been dating miss Bitterman from just down the road and from what I hear it's pretty serious. Mason is all tied up with Dorothy and I need men that can keep their mind on what they're doing and not be thanking about things they could be doing."

"Aren't you just about in the same shape? After all, you're married with a couple of kids. Don't you think about them when you're out for people like Ms. Carter, or is the only time you think Rachel and those kids is when you're home?"

"That's different, and you know it general, this is my job, Rachel knows that. It is not Andrews and Mason's job. They may have the experience in fighting but they most certainly do not have control over their feelings. Now if you don't want to let me have two extra men then forget it. And I'll go after her by myself."!!

Without saying another word. Hightower got up, put his hat on, and walked out the door headed to the barn. Even though the general called his name and told him to stop Hightower was highly peeved and not in the mood to listen to anyone, besides the general had no jurisdiction over, Edward Hightower, US Marshall. When Hightower walked into the barn Andrews and Mason and Lewis were standing there and Hightower could tell by the looks on her face that Lewis had already told them what he said. Taking off his hat and taking off his gun belt Hightower turned around, looked at all three men and said, "I've changed my mind. I'm not going to allow any of you to go with me to bring in Elizabeth Carter. My reasons are this, I want three men backing me up, that can keep their mind on what they're doing. The only one of the three of you that is not tied up in a romance is Lewis, but because the three of you are extremely good friends, I won't take one and leave two."

Andrew spoke up and said, "what about your wife. Hightower as you say you're in romance yourself, so what makes you different than us." "Because this is my job. Andrews, not your. So as far as I'm concerned, your involvement concerning the Carter gang is over and done with. If you still want to guard my family and keep them safe that's okay with me, at least here you will have more than adequate support."

Then Hightower turned to the old man that took care of the stables and ask him, "would you be so good Sir, as to saddle Comanche for me and work me up a pack animal. I don't think I have to tell you what to put on the pack animal I'm pretty sure you already know. If you can have both horses ready to go within an hour." The old timer looked up at Hightower and said, "I'll have her done, Sir, but I got to say that I think you're wrong by not taking these three gentlemen. I once heard you say, Sir, that you would ride through hell with these three men backing you up. What changed Sir? All they did was fall in love, and in my way of thinking that gives a man more of an incentive to come back, because he's got something to look forward to, maybe I'm crazy, but that's the way I see things."!!

When Hightower turned around, he was surprised to find Rachel, Dorothy, and miss. Bitterman standing there in the doorway of the barn and it looked as if they were about to go bear hunting with a switch, and it looked like Hightower was the bear.

Miss Bitterman was the first one to speak, she spoke very little, but what she said him home "Kenneth and I have already talked about this, and we agree this is something he has to do, not only to help you Sir, but to help him repay a kindness to a very distinguished man. Kenneth believes that he owes this and much more to the judge for his kindnesses and for his willingness to stand up for what's right. So don't deny him, Mr. Hightower, the right to do the right thing." Rachel and Dorothy looked at each other and then they looked directly into Hightower's eyes and the two sisters said the same thing at the same time, "we agree with miss Bitterman wholeheartedly."! Hightower turned around and looked at Andrews and the young man was leaned up against a stall door with a big smile on his face and finally he said, "well, it looks like your kind of outnumbered Edward. When do we leave boss?"

"Tomorrow morning, gentlemen, day break. We can't wait any longer. She could have already replaced the men she lost, but maybe not and the fewer we have to go up against the better were going to be. We do need to go by the Indian village. I want to pick up a good Indian scout. Not that I can't do the job, but it's hard to watch the horizon and the ground at the same time, because sooner or later you're going to miss something, and it may get you killed. Get your gear squared away. You need two 45s and a Winchester, with plenty of ammunition. Get the freshest and fastest mounts that you have, and for God sakes find useful jeans and shirts, so that you can look like Cowboys instead of troopers if you've got regular boots, then wear them. Old timer do you have three horses here that does not have a US cavalry brand on them?" "Yes Sir, got three came in yesterday, they ain't branded yet, and there only about half broke, but I got three horses.

Hightower looked at the three men and said, "pick out one piece and get him saddled and start riding. They need to be pretty much broke by tomorrow morning." "You can forget about saddling Comanche, and the pack horses, at least tonight. But they'll need to be saddled by daybreak tomorrow morning." "No problem," the old timer said, then, just as a needle to irritate Hightower in fun. The old man said with a smile, "boss". Hightower just looked at Andrews and turned around and walked off toward the ranch house with Rachel holding on to his arm. The last thing Hightower heard from the three men was Lewis saying, "damn, I guess this means I got to find me a woman, then he heard miss Bitterman say " I've got just the friend for you. "Hightower thought to himself, "my God somewhere down the line I have joined the petticoat parade."!!

Walking back toward the ranch house, Rachel squeezed Hightower's arm and looked at him with a great big smile and said, "now don't you feel better Edward?" "Yeah, I do, but I don't want them to find out. If they do find out, then I'll know you told them, and then my do-gooder wife you will get your bottom spanked, bare butt." "Edward Hightower," Rachel said with a coy little grin on her face, "you got me, trembling in my boots." Then she hiked up her dress to her knees and took off running toward the ranch house, all the while she was saying, "bet you can't catch me."

Just as Rachel reached the front porch. She stopped and turned around, lowering her dress and brushing it as if to get all of the wrinkles out of it and stood there looking down the lane, so Hightower turned and looked up and there was a buckboard headed up to the house. It was the funeral direction and the preacher.

Hightower continued walking at a slow pace, because with the preacher and the undertaker there at the house. There was no reason for him to chase his wife, at this time. Hightower thought to himself, "undertaker's and preachers always seem to show up at the word possible times."

When he walked into the house. The undertaker and the preacher looked a little stoned faced as if they didn't know what to expect. Hightower broke the ice saying, "I really didn't think you two would show up till tomorrow morning, but being you're here go ahead and take care of business." Then he continued walking back to the kitchen, poured him a cup of coffee and set down with a cup of coffee, a pad of paper and a pencil. He decided he was going to make a list of things that his wife would need to have done by the hired help around the ranch while he was gone. As he sat there writing he thought back to when he was a kid and how his father had met and married Elizabeth, it's was a good life for a while, until Raymond got old enough to bully smaller kids, and Elizabeth refused to punish him for anything he done, and would throw a fit whenever his dad corrected Raymond. So eventually it came down to the point when Raymond turned 17 that it was either Raymond leaves home, or him and his dad did. That led to the night that his father and him took only what they needed along with a wagon and two horses, and left everything else behind, including Elizabeth. He had been forced back into Elizabeth's life, because of Raymond's outlaws spree and his eagerness to kill innocent people. Judge Tatum, along with the pull from the general Whitehead, had been responsible for this US marshals badge being penned on his chest, and his first orders was to bring in Raymond Carter, of which he did. Not long after that Raymond was hung for murder and bank robbery, that hanging started all the trouble with Elizabeth Carter. Now, his orders were to bring in Elizabeth Carter alive, if possible.

Dead, if there is no other way, "but bring her in." All of this had Hightower, so entranced in his thoughts that he never noticed when the preacher and the undertaker left, or when Rachel came into the kitchen until he was shocked back to reality when she placed her hands on Hightower shoulders from behind and kissed him on the cheek. She had surprised him so much that he jumped and spilled his coffee all over the kitchen table and accidentally bumped her on the chin with his head. His actions took Rachel so much by surprise that when he bumped her chin with his head she stumbled backwards against the wall losing her footing and setting down on the kitchen floor, flat on her fanny. Her eyes were wide open in surprise as she stared at Hightower. Then her surprise seem to fade and her facial expressions changed into a smile and then she began to laugh saying, "I meant to get your attention, not scare the hell out of you."

Hightower reached down and help her up, he immediately apologized and making sure that she wasn't hurt. Then he kissed her on the chin, on the cheek, on her forehead, then he started to pull back and Rachel put her arms around his neck and said with a girlish tone to her voice. "You forgot these and then she kissed him on the lips with enough passion to make the blood boil in a dead man.!!!

Suddenly they were interrupted by Dorothy coming back through the front door at a very fast walk and she was calling Rachel's name in a high pitched voice, so naturally Rachel thought something was wrong, and responded by saying, "I'm in the kitchen. Dorothy, my God girl what's wrong?" Dorothy stuck out her left hand and said, "he ask me Rachel, he finally ask me." Rachel put her hands on her hips and looked at Dorothy very questioningly, "who ask you what?"

"Mason, Dorothy said he finally got up the nerve to ask me to marry him, and I said yes. We're going to be married, just as soon as this Elizabeth Carter fiasco is over and done with, and I am quite sure Edward that he wants to ask you to be his best man, but I told him, you couldn't be his best man, because I want you to give me away."

Hightower very pleased but not wanting to show it, sat back down in his chair and rubbed his chin and ask, "are you really sure you want me to do that, as much stuff that I have messed up here lately it might not be a good idea."

Then Dorothy pulled up a chair next to Hightower and said, "you are one of the reasons why he asked me to marry him, oh he loves me, there's no doubt about that, and there's no doubt in my mind, he will make a good husband and a good father, but he is also a good friend. He explained to me that another reason for us to get hitched was because he didn't believe that if you two were intended in-laws that you would refuse to allow him to help you bring in Elizabeth Carter. He thinks the world of you Edward, he told me that to him. You were the big brother that he never had, and he wants to do everything he can to make sure your around to teach our children about respect for your fellow man, respect for your parents, and respect for the law. And he wants you to be the godfather of our first child."

"Well, I think maybe you might get a little bit of working experience with children because if I'm not mistaken, I hear at least one baby in there in the bedroom, and being that Rachel is not breast-feeding anymore, maybe you can give her a hand with the babies, because they can be fed the same time with a bottle. But now I want to say something Dorothy, I don't want you and Mason to wait for the ending of Elizabeth Carter, I want you to go out there, find Mason and tell him to go get preacher right now. Dorothy Mason, it's got a nice ring to it, don't you think Rachel?"

Dorothy jumped up and sprinted out the front door all the time saying, "I'll be back in just a moment to help you feed the babies." "I don't believe that she touched a step on that front porch, and if I haven't lost my mind. I believe she jumped over the railing with a dress on,!! "Rachel said with a smile that seemed to cover her whole face. Then she picked up two baby bottles and headed for the bedroom. She had just gone through the bedroom door, when Dorothy came back through the front door at a dead run and slid when she tried to stop in the hallway, but didn't fall, she simply caught the door facing and swung into the bedroom.

Having cleaned up his mess and got another cup of coffee, Hightower leaned back in his chair and in the quiet of the kitchen, he pictured in his mind's eye a family of law abiding citizens, well mannered children, and a strong willed women. Life couldn't be better.?

Hightower felt a swelling of pride in his chest, so with his arms stretched up over his head. He interlaced his fingers placed his hands on back of his head and leaned back in the chair, but he leaned just a little too far.

All, Rachel and Dorothy heard was a big crash in the kitchen and then a whole fistful of cuss words. As Hightower picked himself and the chair up off the floor. Embarrassed to tell the ladies that he had fell backwards in a chair. He just said, "damn it, I tripped over my own Spurs, I shouldn't have these things own in the house anyway."

Rachel and Dorothy knowing what had happened sat on the edge of the bed, each with a baby and it took everything they had to keep from breaking out in a gut wrenching laugh, but they both realized that laughter at this very moment would not be a good thing.

Having had all the surprises that he could stand in one day, Hightower headed for the living room and the liquor cabinet. Getting him a glass and pouring more than half a glass of whiskey. He set down. Just as the front door opened and in walked Mason, Lewis, and Andrews. Hightower held his glass up to them and then nodded in the direction of the liquor cabinet telling them it was all right to fix themselves and drink. Then Hightower looked at Andrews and ask," where's miss Bitterman?" "I already took her back home, boss. I really hope what she said down at the barn didn't make you mad. Actually, she told me to tell you that miss Bitterman was her Mama, her name is Katie, and I think she likes you just a little bit, boss."

As the three men set down in a circle Hightower spoke up. "Tomorrow morning, I want you three men in cowboy clothes, boots and all, and I want these penned on your chest," he then pitched each man a small velvet covered box. "We'll meet here at five in the morning for breakfast, I want to be on the trail as the sun comes up and you need to be prepared for a long trip and I would really enjoy it. If you wound join us for supper this evening. Now that's enough shop talk how about a few hands of poker?

For the next two hours, the four men set at the card table playing poker and sipping some good Kentucky bourbon. Then Andrew stood up and said, "I would really like to join you for supper, but I promised Katie I would spend this evening with her, so if you gentlemen will excuse me, I'm going to make sure that Katie misses me as much as I'm going to miss her."

Hightower looked at Andrews and said, "don't forget 5 o'clock in the morning. In your cowboy clothes and you are to have nothing on you that can be linked to the U.S. Army, and make sure that you got plenty of ammunition at least one change of clothes, preferably two if you got them. Everything else that we'll need should be on the back horse."

"Looks like it's going to be you and Lewis, Mason said. Because I plan on spending this evening with Dorothy." Lewis spoke up and said, "there is a cute little waitress who's single and works at the restaurant beside the hotel in town, and we've been seeing each other off and on. I think this evening will be a good time to go see her, how about you boss?, Don't you think it would be a good evening to spend with you wife and babies?"

"Yes, I do Alan. Hightower said." Hightower, that's the first time you ever call me by my first name. I wasn't even sure that you knew what it was."

"I've known for quite some time. I was just trying to keep from getting too close. But my wife who seems to be the smart one in this family has decided that you three gentlemen, and I are friends. So friends get called by first names, so until five in the morning. Kenneth , Alan, Will, I guess I'm going to act like something that I haven't acted like in quite a while, And I'm ashamed of myself for admitting it. I'm going to act like a husband and a father, there is one other thing I want to tell you we have to make plain right now. I would sure like when all of this is over with, and everyone comes back that we get together along with the troopers in the stockade, including the general for an extremely large cookout. I think that I can spare a beef to be put on the spit, and I might even talk Mr. Dean into doing the cooking, so that the ladies can dress up, spruce up, and get all of their feminine ways in order. Hope fully by the time this happens, it will not be Edward and Rachel Hightower, but Kenneth and Katie Andrews, Will and Dorothy Mason, and last but not least Alan and what ever that young waitresses name is, Lewis. So when we leave here gentlemen, I want one thing on everybody's mind, the arrest of Elizabeth Carter and her gang." Hightower raised his glass and said, "here's to getting the job done, quickly, and completely, and as safely as possible."

All four men turned their glasses up and downed. What ever whiskey was left turned their glasses upside down on the card table. Kenneth and Alan left out the front door, while Mason went out the back door. Leaving just Rachel and the babies in the house, because Dorothy went out the back door with Mason, accidentally letting the back door slam it woke up the twins. Rachel looked over at Hightower, smiled and said, "we'll talk later on tonight."

Being that Rachel was tied up with the babies, Hightower decided to walk out onto the front porch and set for a spell. He was setting there doing nothing. When Andrew and Katie came riding through the main gate and headed for the ranch house. Andrew got off of his horse and said, "Katie said you were good enough to invite everyone to supper and it would be rude not to accept." He then walked around to Katie's pony and took the reins and tied it to the hitching post, and helped her down. Katie smiled at Hightower and said, "besides, I'm quite sure that Rachel could stand some help with the children. I'm surprised that the babies aren't out here on the porch lying on their blanket just waiting for their father to play with them.

Hightower, smiled and said, "they were asleep until Dorothy went out the back door with Mason and accidentally let the door slam. That's where Rachel is now trying to get them back down to sleep so she can get supper fixed. I have no idea where Mason and Dorothy went, you can go look for them. If you want to."

Katie looked at Andrew and said, "I'm going inside and see if there's anything I can do to help Rachel. Why don't you stay out here and talk to Edward for a while, I'm sure you have some plans to make and things to discuss." "It seems that were going to be here for a spell. So if you don't mind boss, I'm going to take the two horses down to the corral and unsaddled them." "That's a good idea. Andrews, you can always use the buckboard to take her back home. Your horse is going to need all the rest he can get."

Hightower set on the porch and watched Andrews as he led both horses down to the corral and unsaddled them, putting both saddles and bridles on the corral fence. The old timer came out and said something to Andrew and whatever it was that he said lit a fire under Andrews feet because he wheeled and ran back up to the house. When he reached the front porch. He looked at Hightower and said, "the old timer in the barn just told me that the chief is in the general's office with one of his Braves, and from what he overheard the Indian is Someone the chief sent to trail Carter and he knows where she's holding up. It seems that you were right boss, she's only got eight men left and two of them are wounded.!

Getting up out of his chair. Hightower stepped on the porch and said, come on, Kenneth Let's go talk to the chief. When the two men entered the general's office, both he and the chief were standing and looking at the general's map of the reservation. The young brave was pointing at an area about 50 miles southwest of Lake Charles in a section of the Bayou that no one knew a whole lot about. The area was extremely secluded and except for a couple of old abandoned fishing camps. There was nothing out there.

The general turned around and motion for Hightower to move on up closer to the map and then he asked, "what do you think Edward? Do you think a squad of men will be enough?" Hightower studied the map for just a moment and then he told the general, "don't need a squad general, the three men that I asked for will be more than enough. She finally made a mistake. The reason why that those fishing camps were abandoned was because there was only one way in, and one way out without a boat, and she damn sure ain't going to put no horse in a canoe. Besides, they could see a squad of troopers coming 2 miles away. Not only will it be hard for them to get out, but it will be next to impossible without suffering great losses for a squad of troopers to try to force their way in. It just ain't gonna happen general. Going out there in that Bayou country's is going to take three or four men and they are going to have to be sneaky as hell. Not only is that Bayou riddled with moccasins but it's over run with gators and their always hungry."!

Hightower continued to explain to the general that they would have to stash their horses somewhere they would be safe and then they needed to come up with two canoes, and then only after dark will they be able to make any kind of a move on Carter and her men. Turning around and looking at the young Indian. Hightower spoke to him in his native language, "I can't order you to do anything, the man took just a second to think, and then the chief told him to do what the man ask. Hightower looked at the chief and said once again speaking Cherokee, "I will not take this man with me, if you order him to go. If he goes. It will be by his own choice, there is no reason for him to put his life on the line for us, if he goes or stays. It will be his choice, not yours, not mine, not even the general's."

"I will take you to the place where they entered the Bayou, but I will not go into the Bayou. Instead I will stay with the horses, and take care of them and if you do not return, I will return them to your ranch."

Andrews put his hand on the young Indians shoulder and said, "you get us that close son and we'll take care of the rest." Hightower looked at

Andrews and then he repeated to the Indian in Cherokee what Andrews had said to him. The young brave smiled and shock his head, showing that he understood. Hightower and Andrews went back to looking at the map and Hightower asked the general, "can you get a message to your man, and have him meet us at this point right here." Hightower picked up a pin and stuck it at a point on the Bayou.

The general turned around, looked at the Cpl. that operated the telegraph and then walked over to his desk picked up a piece of paper and a pencil, wrote something down and handed it to the Cpl. and said, "send this, just the way it is written; don't add anything, don't leave anything out,"!!! When do you think you can meet him Hightower?" "If we leave at first light we should be able to be there about dark. If you would general send him another wire and give him the location and tell him to set up camp when he gets there, that way he'll be a lot easier for us to find. If when we reach that location he's not there yet. Then we'll set up camp and he can find us."

Hightower, then turned to the chief and asked the chief, "do you have any Braves the size of my men?" He put his hand on Andrews shoulder and made him turn around and show the chief his back in the length of his arms, and then he pointed at the chief's buckskins and moccasins telling him that he needed three sets and he would be more than glad to pay for them. The chief looked at the young Indian brave and told him to go get three sets, including moccasins and bring them back as quickly as possible. The young brave jumped up and ran out the door and as if he had springs in his legs jumped on his horse and was gone in less time than it took to tell someone what had happened.

Andrews looked at Hightower and said, "aren't you going to wear buckskins boss?" Hightower looked at him with a grin and said, "I've got my own set and I have also got a pair of Apache boots and to pair of Comanche moccasins. Up until now I haven't had an occasion to wear anything but the buckskin pants and then I have only worn them, maybe three times."

"I'm going back up to the house and sit and talk to Katie while she helped Rachel, Andrew said." Raising his hand. Hightower said, "wait just a second and I'll go with you."

Chapter 7

When Hightower stepped out onto the front porch at a quarter till five in the morning, he found three men dressed in buckskin's and four saddled horses, and one pack horse being held by the old timer that took care of the stables, Sgt. brothers. After everyone had said, "good morning boss," the instigator who seem to be tickled pink to get Hightower's blood running first thing in the morning Sgt. brothers said, "I don't think I've forgotten anything, but you might want to check and make sure because I've never loaded a pack horse for you and I'm not accustomed to the way you travel, but what's on this horse is what I would take.

As Hightower was checking out the pack horse, Dorothy came to the door and said, "okay, gentlemen breakfast is ready." Looking over at the old Sgt. Hightower said, "if you would care to join us Sgt., you're more than welcome." "No, Sir, he said, this is a very special breakfast, and it only stands to reason that one, or more of you will never eat breakfast at this table again. I sincerely hope that I am wrong, but I have seen a lot of good men go down. I took over the job of taking care of the horses, not so much because I couldn't ride and shoot anymore, but because I was tired of watching friends die. So I beg your leave sir, maybe when you come back, I'll join you then. The old Sgt. stuck out his hand to each one of the men, and said, "May all of your angles in heaven ride with you and keep you safe. It's all up to the good Lord now." Then he turned and walked away, right before he disappeared into the barn he turned and looked back. He didn't wave, he didn't tip his hat, he just looked and then disappeared from sight.

"I don't want any of you men to get it in your head that you're going to die if we do this right and with just a little bit of luck were going to be able to pull this off without anyone getting hurt. I'll explain everything to you as we ride and then we'll go over the whole thing again. When we make camp, or meet up with the Cajun late this evening. Now, lets eat before it gets cold, I believe it's steak and eggs, biscuits and gravy with plenty of hot coffee."

When the four men walked into the kitchen. They found three women there, Rachel, Dorothy, and Katie, who had spent the night. Unbeknown to Andrews, just so she could see him off and let him know beyond a doubt that he had something to come back to. Hightower could read in her eyes that she didn't really want him to go, but she knew that he wanted to go, he wanted to help end the reign of terror by this crazy, evil, woman.

The four men set down at the breakfast table and they sort of resembled some of the men who fought with Hightower in the Indian wars. The buckskins fit the men perfectly, and so did their moccasins. It was then that Lewis noticed Hightower still had his boots on and ask, "how come you still got your boots?" "I was going to tell you gentlemen that it's a lot easier riding with your boots on than with the moccasins, so if you want to put your boots on before we leave It's okay, just stick the moccasins in your saddlebags. You'll put them back on before we go into the Bayou."

When breakfast was over. Andrews, Lewis, and Mason hotfootedit back down to the bunkhouse where they had been staying and slipped their boots on and came back very quickly and put their moccasins in their saddlebags. Then, Hightower told the men, "if you want to you can take a few minutes and say goodbye to your ladies. I know I most assuredly am going to spend a few moments with my wife. You've got 15 minutes, go."

Hightower took Rachel by the hand and led he back into the house, he then sat her down on the sofa and said, "Rachel, if everything goes the way I think it will, and we bring Elizabeth back and as many of her men as we possibly can, what do you think about me turning this badge in? I really think it's time that I became a full-time husband and father, and started taking care of this ranch instead of chasing all over the country. I have missed a lot of time with you and the children that I can never get back, I really don't want to miss anymore."

Looking deep into Hightower's eyes. Rachel said, "Edward, sweetheart, you know as well as I do, that badge is as much a part of you as I am. If you gave up that badge somewhere down the line you would resent me for allowing you to remove it, so no Edward, I don't want you to take that badge off, it's who you are, and besides you have done a lot of good for the people. You mustn't ever stop being the man who stands up for the ones who can't." Then she put her arms around his neck and kissed him very passionately, when their lips parted, she said, "now, Mr. Hightower, you go take care of business and don't worry about the children and I. we'll be just fine, after all, we have got a full troop of cavalry watching over us.

Hightower stood up, looked Rachel dead in the eye and said, "I love you lady, I know sometimes I don't say that when I really should, but I'm saying it now and I fully intend from now on it will be the first thing I say to you every morning. and the last thing I say to you every night." Then he kissed her again and turned and walked out the front door, as he stepped onto the porch in a loud voice. He said. "the suns up. Let's ride."!...............

It took a couple or more minutes for Andrews and Mason to get mounted. Lewis had set patiently on his horse watching all of the goodbyes that were being said, so Hightower slapped him on the shoulder and said, "when you get back. Lewis, I want you to go into town and have a good long talk with that little waitress, it would be kind of nice to have a triple wedding here on the ranch. You know a life as a farmer and small rancher is not bad when you have a woman, and some kids had depend on you and love you. It's a mighty good feeling to know that the only time you will be using a rifle is to occasionally take down a deer."

"I've already done just that boos. The last time I seen her, we talked. She said that she had just about given up on me asking her, anyway boss, she said yes." "I understand why you're so calm and relaxed now, you've already said your goodbyes." Hightower said.

Three women were lined up on the front porch, when the four men turned their horses away from the house and said goodbye one time. The sun had just started peeking over the Eastern horizon, so Hightower and his band of merry men would be riding with the sun in their faces.

Waiting in a stand of trees southwest of the house was the young brave that would be leading them. When he came out of the trees, he took the lead and set a pace that his Indian pony could hold on to all day. Hightower notice that the young brave had brought what he had asked for and they were tied across the back of his pony. Four Bow's, and four quivers of arrows. They would be the ideal weapons, if they could just get close enough.

The first three hours of their ride went easy, then the Indian stopped his pony and dismounted knelt down and motioned for Hightower to join him. Walking over and kneeling down the Indian took his hand and showed Hightower, a horseshoe print. Then standing up the young brave pointed in the direction of a large stand of trees and then in Cherokee, he said. "Crazy woman and her followers go into trees ride around and come back out, go that way." He was pointing due South, straight to the Bayou on the border of Louisiana and Texas. An unforgiving place that only the ones who used to fish it dare go into. If you ever get lost in that Bayou the chances that you will find your way out is not very good.

Hightower and the young Indian remounted and continued heading south with the young brave in the lead.

Twice during the afternoon, little Trees, which Hightower had learned was the young braves name, had stopped and checked the trail on foot and changed directions each time. Late that evening. As they neared the point where they were to meet the general's friend named Apollo, the young brave stopped and motion for Hightower one more time. As Hightower rode up beside him. Little trees pointed off to the left at a small stream of smoke rising quietly and so faint that only a Indian expecting to see it, would see it. Patting little trees on the shoulder, Hightower pointed at the smoke and told him that was where they was headed. Little trees headed off in that direction slowly, and cautiously. He wanted to be sure that this was the man they were supposed to meet, and not the crazy woman.

Hightower turned around and looked at his three comrades to tell them to get their Winchesters out and be ready, but he was a little too late. They were already carrying their Winchesters in their hand, and with a simple nod of their heads. They told Hightower, they were ready for whatever came their way. When they were close enough to the camp to see it. Hightower motioned for little trees and the others to stay down and wait for his signal. Riding up to the camp. Hightower paused and in a loud clear voice said, "you in the camp, can I come in?" A voice with a French accent said, "if you name be Hightower, come on in. If your name not be Hightower, you best go away, okay."

Hightower urged the big gray forward and as he neared the campfire the Frenchman stood up, holding a rifle and Hightower said, "I'll be Hightower, if you're Apollo. Immediately the Frenchman lowered his rifle and said, "you make good time my friend, tell your men to come on in, they are welcome." Turning around in his saddle. Hightower gave the signal for the other men to come into camp.

The Frenchman had already set up camp and had a whole stringer of fish already caught and cleaned, and ready to fix Cajun style. Almost immediately little trees and Apollo started carrying on a conversation discussing where Apollo thought Carter and her men would be. That's when Apollo told little trees that he would lead them into the Bayou. Just to make sure that they came back out alive. Little trees told Apollo that he had agreed to lead them this far and then to stay with the heroes, and take care of the campsite. Hightower couldn't understand completely what Apollo was saying, but was something like, "good idea, you stay, you not know Bayou like Apollo." That was more or less the jest of the conversation, which to Hightower made a lot of sense. Apollo was born and raised in these Bayou's, and he knew how to travel through the Bayou silently, but quickly. It seemed that the trust that this young man had in general Whitehead was paying off. What ever had brought this man, and general Whitehead together. Hightower would sure love to find out what he did to deserve such loyalty. Maybe another day and another glass of whiskey and he'd ask the general, but right now it was time to eat and then get some rest before starting into the Bayou and the final meeting with Elizabeth Carter!!!.....

Sgt. brothers had put a half a dozen plates and the same amount of forks in a bag on the pack horse, along with a coffee pot, and coffee, sugar, salt and pepper. There were eight blankets. One to sleep on, one to cover up with. While Apollo and little trees prepared the fish Mason made a pot of coffee, Lewis scouted around trying to find enough wood to keep the fire burning, or at least keep live coals so that we could have coffee in the morning before we started into the Bayou. Andrews unsaddled the four horses, and the pack horse and placed the saddles around the campfire, where every man would sleep. By the time they had gotten everything done the fish was ready to eat and all six men set down in a circle and ate until they couldn't eat anymore. They had allowed the horses to graze and get their fill of water, then each man picketed his horse and took turns brushing the horses down, simply because they only had one brush between them.

Little trees had decided he would stand the first watch so Apollo would be up and ready when it came time to venture off into the Bayou. He had explained to Hightower and the other three just how they were going to go about getting close enough to these people to capture them with the least amount of danger. When he started talking to Hightower. It didn't take Apollo long to figure out that he was not talking to a greenhorn. It was evident that Hightower had been down this road before and so had the three men that were riding with him. As the men started to bed down, After brushing their horses out Apollo said, "we need to go into Bayou before sun comes up. It best to travel in darkness, but fight in daylight."

"What ever time you think we need to get up, just wake us up, okay, you have no idea how much I have looked forward to this day. Elizabeth Carter and her gang had a lot of things to pay up for, and I fully intent to make sure that she pays for every evil thing she's done. All of the murders, the bank robberies, all of the pain that she has caused innocent people. I intend to make sure she pays for every evil deed." "You really do not like this woman, do you?" Apollo ask! Andrew spoke up and ask Apollo, "do you by any chance know judge Tatum in Lake Charles?" "Yes, the judge is an honorable man and a friend to the people in the Bayou, why do you ask if I know the judge?" "This woman and the men who ride with her murdered the judge and his wife while they were setting on the front porch. They shot them down in cold blood."

"I did not know that, Apollo said, now I will be more than glad to help you bring them out of the Bayou and I will be more than glad to tie the rope that hangs them, but I would rather cut their throats while they sleep!!"

"I know how you feel, Apollo. I have no love whatsoever for this woman myself, but I am an officer on the law and I am sworn to uphold the law and everyone is entitled to be treated the same way. The law says that you are innocent until proven guilty in a court of law and judged by a jury of your peers. I am charged by the law, not only to arrest this woman, but also protect her until she can go to court. Now, Apollo if you feel that you won't be able to restrain your self and you are planning on trying to kill her, then not only will you not go into the Bayou with us. I will have to ask you to leave. So you make up your mind, do you obey the law or not?"

"Wee, my friend, I will obey the law, even though it will not be easy," Apollo said.! Hightower turned to Little Trees and made the same statement to him in Cherokee. The young brave answered Hightower saying, "only my chief has the right to take this woman's life, because she took the life of his son. He has sent me to help you bring her to the white man's court and as you are sworn by the law, so am I sworn by the word of my chief. I promise I will not harm the crazy woman in any way."

"Keep that fire burning, so we can see the smoke, the smoke will lead us back here, and you must be ready to move as quickly as possible. There will be a lot of people out after this woman's life for what she done to the judge and his wife, so we have to get to Lake Charles, As quickly as possible."

Andrews ask Hightower, "somebody is going to have to bring those horses out of the Bayou, we can't just leave them in there to be slaughtered by the gators. And it really depends on how many of them, we can take alive to how many horses were going to need. I suggest that the rest of the horses be given to little trees as payment for his help, what do you think boss?" "That sounds like a good idea Kenneth, but it's not likely that any of those men will lead you out of the swamp, Knowing that there's an awful good chance that they're going to hang.

Apollo spoke up saying, "I will bring the horses out by myself or with one of your men. It makes no difference to me. I too do not think the horses should be left, the horses are not evil just their riders."

Hightower stood up and took off his gun belt and the said, "all right then, everyone knows what were going to do in the morning, as of right now I would suggest that everyone lay down and at least rest, those of you who can go to sleep. I suggest you do just that. After we have Elizabeth and as many of her men as we can capture then, and only then, will we worry about the horses, but to ease your mind. I never intended to leave them, I couldn't. I could never bring myself to be cruel to an animal that I respect so much."

Little Trees began stoking up the fire and then he made the rounds, checking the horses and going over the surrounding area and then he set down crosslegged on a blanket with a Winchester cradled inn his arms. Then he went through a Cherokee chant that in fact was the same as a small prayer to keep everyone safe while watching him. Hightower simply smiled and nodded his head to the young Indian and little trees returned the same nod and smile to Hightower.

It didn't seem like any time at all until Apollo was waking everyone up by kicking them on the bottom of the feet. Hightower set up and because he had been startled from a deep sleep. He said, "what is it? What's wrong?" Apollo jumped back and said, "nothing's wrong, it is just time to wake up. I have already made coffee.

Apollo had gotten the same reaction from Andrews, Lewis and Mason. Little trees was still sitting crosslegged and holding his Winchester with a big smile on his face. He looked at Hightower and for the first time the young brave spoke a broken English saying, "white man dream about sqauw, talking in sleep all night."

Hightower looked at the young Indian and smiled and said jokingly, "why, you sneaky little devil you, I'm going to have to keep an eye on you. I didn't think you spoke any English at all, you sure had me fooled." Little trees spoke again, saying, "white man should not trust so much, but rely on sensus more."

It was still dark, and it was still going to be a couple of hours before it even acted like it was going to get daylight. So after the men had a couple of cups of coffee and replaced their boots with the moccasins. They loaded their weapons into the two canoes that Apollo had managed to come up with. Each man carried four strips of inch wide rawhide, they didn't have cuffs, so they would use the rawhide to bind the outlaws hands, if need be.

Apollo, Hightower, and Mason were in the lead canoe Lewis and Andrews were in the second canoe and everyone had been told to stay as quiet as possible because sound traveled very fast over the waters in the Bayou. A rope had been tied from the back of the lead canoe to the front of the second canoe, so they couldn't get separated.

With a simple wave of his hand. Apollo started off, and with the appearance of a large snake cutting through water, the two canoes disappeared into the Bayou, never making a sound.

The first fishing camp they came to was deserted. Carter and her gang had to be at the second camp, which was about 2 miles deeper into the Bayou. So Apollo led off again, this time, slower and even more quite. I took about a half hour to cover the 2 miles and sure enough they were there. Beaching the canoe's very gently, and getting out of the canoes one man at a time, making sure they did not step into the water and make splash. The five men made their way to the camp and there in a circle asleep around a fire was six men. Apollo nudged Hightower on the arm and pointed off to his right, there was two fresh graves, evidently the last two men hit by Dorothy and Rachel shotguns didn't make it. But Hightower motioned for everyone to stay put. There were some buildings that he had to check out. The building furthest away was the first one Hightower checked, it was a good thing that he did. There, curled up on the floor was Elizabeth Carter Asleep, She looked like any ordinary woman with the moonlight shining on her face. Very cautiously Hightower stepped into the room with his 45 drawn, all of a sudden he noticed, there was someone else lying on the floor and he had very silently set up and only the glint of the moonlight reflecting off of his 45 had saved Hightower. Without hesitation his 45, bucked in his hand and the man was forcibly slammed back on the floor by the force of the 45 in the same motion. Hightower had dropped down on one knee next to Elizabeth and had taken the Winchester that was lying next to her away.

Grabbing the blanket that she was covered with he jerked it away and it was a good thing he did, because she already had her hand on a 45 that was under the cover. Putting his hand on the weapon and pulling it away. He then clipped her on the jaw and said, I never have been much for walkin round barefooted, especially in the woods where there's snakes a crawlin and all kinds of things that can stick right through the bottom one of those moccasins. No thank you, Sir, but I'll take my boots any day."

"I know exactly how you feel Mason, the first time I put a pair on I hollored ouch more than a few times, but Hightower said, it didn't take me long to get used to wearing them, especially when I was trying to sneak up on an Indian during the wars."

"How long are we going to set here boss?" Kenneth, were going to set here for a long as it takes Apollo to get them horses here so if anyone knows anything about fixing breakfast I would suggest getting started. What's on that pack horse? Sgt. Brown said he packed what he would take, somebody take a look and see if he packed anything to eat," Hightower said as he was getting Elizabeth out of the canoe. Her hands were already tied behind her, and she had not shut up since she had woke up so Hightower took his bandanna and tied it to cover her mouth. Then he tied a piece of rawhide around her ankles mainly to keep her from trying to run.

He looked at Elizabeth and said, "Elizabeth. When you can calm down a little bit and stopped running that mouth I'll take the gag off, I might even take the rawhide off of your ankles, but I will not take any chances with you. Too many others have, and it's cost them their lives I've spent the better part of two years chasing you and in that time I have seen at least 20 people buried because of you. Granted, most of them were members of your gang, but I can name seven that were not. You're going back to Lake Charles where all of this started and you're going to pay the piper."

Lewis, let out a holler, saying, "there's Apollo boss with all of the horses, do you still want someone to fix breakfast?" "Yes, I do, I'm in no mood to ride all day without having something to eat."

"We've got a big slab of bacon and some beans, there's some flour, so we can make some biscuits." Mason said. "Well I guess it's up to me to cook, Lewis said, after all, I'm the only one not doing anything. Of course, if you're not afraid of getting poisoned boss, you could let Elizabeth fixed breakfast." Andrews and Hightower both at the same time said the same thing, "hell no"!!.....

Aw come on, gentlemen, I'll fix you a breakfast like no breakfast you ever had, Elizabeth said" Hightower looked over at Mason and Lewis and said, "I'm almost sorry now that I removed her gag. I think Lewis, that we can stomach your cooking at least once. The next meal we eat will be in Lake Charles and maybe your lady will wait on us, how does that sound?"

Apollo dismounted from the lead horse and walked over and took a long look at Elizabeth. Then he squatted down and ask her, "are you the person that is responsible for the death of my friend, judge Tatum and his wife Amy?" Not knowing whether to answer or not. Elizabeth never offered a response just a strong evil look came over her face and she spit in Apollo's face. Hightower grabbed Apollo before he could move. What Apollo said in his native tongue, Hightower didn't understand, but Little Trees evidently did, because he started laughing and said something back to Apollo.

"On second thought, forget about any kind of breakfast, just get them horses saddles and lets head for Lake Charles, "Now."! Hightower looked at Mason and said, "I want you to ride along with Little Trees till he gets back to his people. I wouldn't want anyone to mistake an Indian leading a trail of ponies as a horse thief. You get him back to his people safe, then go buy the ranch and let the women know that were headed for Lake Charles we've got Elizabeth. Do not bring the women to town, but you hot foot it to Lake Charles as fast as you can. I've got a feeling, when we get to Lake Charles were going to have a battle just trying to keep Elizabeth alive long enough for her to go before the judge and be formally charged with the murder of the judge and his wife. I can't stress this enough Mason get back with us as fast as you can we're going to need another gun!!"

Being that all of the horses were saddled Apollo took the one that he had ridden out of the Bayou and tethered it along side the horses that Hightower and his men had ridden into this camp.

Little Trees grab hold of the first horse's tether line, then swung up on to his pony and said, "if we leave now and ride at good gallop. We can be with my people, just after the sun is high. That should let you be in Lake Charles before sun goes down."

Mason looked at Hightower and said, "I'll get back with you, Just as quick as I can boss. Are you really sure you want me to go by the ranch,? It just might be a good idea to leave the women out of this until Elizabeth is safely housed behind bars."

"On second thought Mason, that's a good point. Just make sure the first part of your journey is a success and then Haul ass for Lake Charles. We're going to ride at an easy gallop, so you should catch up with us before we get to Lake Charles. I'd sure appreciate it Mason. If you'd try to do just that."

Mason took off to catch up with Little Trees who was wasting no time, the way he was acting he'd had enough of white man for one day.

Everyone else, including Elizabeth was already in the saddle. Hightower told Apollo, "you know the best way to Lake Charles, take the lead and keep us away from as many people as you possibly can. We don't need to have to fight the locals out here in the open, we're on the last legs on this ordeal, so let's get it done, it's been a long time, but there's still a ways to go."

Andrews straightened up his hat pulled out his 45 and checked it to make sure that he had reloaded it. When he placed it back into his holster. He looked at Hightower and said, "like you said boss, let's get it over with."

Nothing else was said by any of the men, but Elizabeth kept saying, "you'll never get me to Lake Charles alive. There are people that are my friends, who will stop you." Then she would laugh that same crazy laugh that Hightower had heard in the ranch house before it burnt, and he thought to himself, "you'll not get away from me this time. Elizabeth, not this time."

Hightower listen to Elizabeth for a little while and then he said, "Elizabeth, I feel sorry for you, simply because I don't believe you're got a friend in this world, you've either had them killed, or killed them yourself, so why don't you just set there on that horse and shut up. I don't want to have to gagged you again." For a little while, at least, Elizabeth was quite but it wasn't long until she stated again and this time Hightower had enough. Getting off of his horse. He went back to Elizabeth and swung up onto the back of her horse, behind her, and gagged her. Dismounting from her horse Hightower said, "my wife made that bandanna for me and now I'm going to have to burn it."!

Climbing back on his horse Hightower positioned himself on the left side of Elizabeth Andrews was on her right side, Lewis was behind her, and Apollo was in front of her. She had nowhere to run, she couldn't even make the horse run by kicking him, because Hightower had placed a noose around the horses neck and so had Andrews. The bridal had been taken off of the horse, so there was no way to her to guide the horse. Just in case she tried to fall off of the horse in an attempt to run her feet had been tied to the stirrups, with rawhide strips.

There was no talking or laughter of any side. Each man was committed to seeing to it that Elizabeth made it back to Lake Charles without a scratch on her, only the bruise on her chin where Hightower had clipped her to keep her quiet and so he could bind her hands. Other than that Elizabeth was in fine shape.

To look at Elizabeth, you would swear she was not big enough to have killed as many men as she had or to have led at least 30 outlaws, the past two years, most of them lie in lonely graves on the side of a trail somewhere in Texas or New Mexico. A few of them are still in the small bayous of Southeast Texas, buried where no one will ever find them. There is nothing but their deeds left that can even mention the even existed.

The sun was getting high in the sky that meant it was getting close to noon, and it also meant that Mason and Little Trees were getting close to his village, at the very least they were on the reservation. Soon Mason would be joining them, and he felt he would have enough firepower just in case anything happened to keep Elizabeth in custody.

It was med afternoon when Apollo led them up to a small ranch house with a watering trough in front and dismounted. A man and a woman and a couple of kids came to the front door and said something in what sounded like French and then gave Apollo, a hug and then pointed at Elizabeth. Apollo spoke for a couple of minutes and the lady turned around and went back into the house with the children and the man followed Apollo backed out to where the horse trough was. Looking up at Hightower. The man spoke in pretty good English, "you are the Marshall Hightower?" Hightower just nodded his head yes, "my brother has asked that you be able to water your horses and rest them for a spell, so get down and water your horses, and then put them in the corral where they can eat.

We have a large Kittle of beef stew freshly made by my wife over the fire and ready to eat. It's not much but you are welcome to share it with us. What are we to do with the woman killer. I would much prefer that she not got into my house and be around my children. "I will stay with her outside, I will eat with her and watch her myself, no one else is to come close to her, except my men and I" Hightower said as he leaned over and offered his hand to the man.

Getting down from his horse, he handed the reins to Lewis and then he untied Elizabeth from the stirrups and helped her down from her horse. Then reluctantly, he took the gag from her mouth and the first thing she said was, "where's the outhouse I'm about to bust wide open?" This was a time that Hightower was dreading, he didn't really know how to handle this. Apollo's brother said, wait just a moment and he hollered something to his wife and then she came out of the door, followed by two other women of equal size, they walked over to Elizabeth, untied her hands, the took hold of her arms and led her to a little buildings just off to the left. They opened the door and took her inside. Hightower watched all four women go into the little buildings no bigger than a good-sized closet. It didn't take very long at all till the women started coming out one at a time. First it was Apollo brothers wife, then Elizabeth. Then the other two women. Hightower noticed that Elizabeth hands were tied again behind her back. When the women brought Elizabeth back over to him, he turned her around and checked the bindings on her wrist. She had been tied by some fancy kind of know, and there was no way that Elizabeth was going to get loose from it. Hightower thanked the ladies for their trouble and then said to Apollo's brothers wife, "she has got to eat. How do I untied that knot?" "You do not have to untie her, I will feed her, I don't want any chances took in feeding that woman, as long as she is here, she will remain bound."!! My two sisters would take care of you and your men. I will take care of the woman with nothing else left to say, she turned around and walked back into the house.

Hightower set Elizabeth down on the edge of the porch and then taking another piece of rawhide he tied her hands while they were behind her back to a porch post, then he leaned back against a post himself and said, "I don't really like treating you like this Elizabeth, but you leave me no choice. If you had only let my father straighten Raymond out years ago, I don't believe that things would have ended up this way. Raymond would not have been hanged, and you most certainly would not be in the shape you're in right now."

By the expression on Elizabeth face Hightower knew there was no reasoning with her. Her whole life over the past two years had been motivated by the hate she had for Hightower. Although he had nothing to do with her son Raymond being hanged, he was the law man who brought him in and turned him over to the Sheriff of Lake Charles Louisiana to be tried on numerous counts of murder and bank robbery. What Elizabeth didn't seem to realize is that if she had stayed on the ranch instead of running and abandoning the ranch, no one would have ever thought of looking for the body of her ex-husband. As far as anyone knew the man had done the same thing that he and his father had done, they had simply just packed up and left. There was no reason whatsoever to think that Mr. Kershaw didn't do the same time. It was a known fact that Elizabeth was not the easiest person in the world to along with. In the time she had lived on that ranch. She had numerous run-ins with neighbors, and there was always a conflict whenever she came into town to buy supply.

When Apollo's sister-in-law brought a plate out to feed Elizabeth, she also brought a plate for Hightower, and as she sat spoon feeding Elizabeth, she told Hightower that the judge had been the one who had married her and her husband, and he had fixed it so that they could buy this little place that they now lived on. She told of how the judge had promised them a better way of life, he had also promised them that their children would be able to get an education and that there would be no reason for them to ever go hungry living this close to the Bayou. The judge out of his own pocket had bought one bull and three heifers so that they could start them a small herd and explained that the cattle would not only be a tremendous source of food, but eventually could provide them with enough money to buy other supplies, or they could even barter with someone in the general store by offering to trade a calf for the supplies that they needed.

It was clear that the mom had felt a deep commitment along with a deep friendship for the judge and his wife. She had learned what kindness meant from the judge and Amy, because she was now passing on that kindness to the killer of her two friends. She spoon fed Elizabeth all that she wanted to eat and then gave her a drink from a large glass of lemonade. When Elizabeth was finished eating and drinking the lady looked her in head in the eye and said, "I hope you rot in hell for what you've done and the people that you have hurt for the sake of a few dollars."

Not knowing what to expect. Hightower kept a sharp eye on the lady. Finally, feeling embarrassed because he didn't know what to call her Hightower tapped her on the shoulder and ask her, "I'm sorry for sounding stupid but ma'am, what is your name? She looked up at Hightower and said, "why do you want to know my name,? You will probably never see me again. You should be like judge Tatum when he met someone and he liked them, he stayed in touch. Even if he had to go out of his way, he stayed in touch.

He and his wife wanted to know if there was anything they could do, or if there was anything you needed, like food or medicine. He would always ask about the children and while he was doing all the talking, Amy was playing with the children or checking them out to make sure they were okay, there was one time that she actually gave my two children, a bath. They were just babies at the time. My son was maybe a year and a half old, my daughter six months old, but she had such a wonderful time with them. I'm going to miss that wonderful lady for a long, long, time."

"I promise, ma'am, if you will tell me what your name is that I will make it a point to stop by here and spend time with you and your husband and your children any time that I am in this area, and being the US Marshall in charge of this area I need to be making the rounds more often. Do you think that you could stand having me, stop by, let's say about once every 10 days? You see I only live about a half a day's ride from here, due North."

Holding her hand up high and with a defiant look on her face, as if she was trying to prove how strong she was, but there was a sparkle in her eye that told Hightower, she wanted to take him at his word, if only to help her remember her two friends. Finally, she said, "my name is Ramona may Willis, my husband's name is Justin Willis, our kids are Joseph and Kaylee."

Then she glanced down at Elizabeth and said, "make her pay for killing my friends." "Oh by the way I guess I need to tell you, I'm married Walter and Amy's oldest daughter Rachel, I thought you should know because maybe someday I'll be able to bring her down to meet you." "She will be welcome anytime, perhaps she can tell me more things about her mother and father."

As she turned to go back into the house, Apollo and his two deputies were coming out. Andrews looked at Hightower and said, "whenever you decide it's time to go, I'll go get the horses." "Well, go get them then, we need to get her mounted up and get on toward Lake Charles."

Chapter 8

There was still plenty of daylight left after the two deputies had gotten Elizabeth into the saddle and once again tied her be to the stirrups. Apollo once again led off into the direction of Lake Charles with both Hightower and Andrews having lead rope's on Elizabeth's horse and Lewis bringing up the rear. The small posse once again started moving, but instead of being at a slow gallop. Hightower had decided to save as much energy in the horses as possible. So for right now, they were simply walking the horses. Of course the big gray did not like the idea walking, but he soon got the idea.

Things went along quietly for quite a spell, but it seemed that the closer they got to Lake Charles, the more vocal Elizabeth got and before long. Hightower had to replace the gag in Elizabeth mouth, but even this did not stop her from running her mouth, although you couldn't understand what she was saying. Hightower could pretty much understand the words because of her actions, and he was pretty sure that most everything she was saying, amounted to a whole lot of four letter words. Finally, after about 10 miles she calmed down and after listening to her rant and rave, quiet sounded even better than usual.

Estimating that the time was about 4 o'clock in the afternoon. Hightower asked Apollo just how many more miles It was to Lake Charles. Apollo answered, "it's not very far on land, but from the angle that we are going to Lake Charles, we will have to take the ferry cross the bay. It's either that or ride for another six hours to go around the Bay. It's up to you which one we do." "Does the furry run all night Apollo?" "Only up until midnight, Apollo answered."

"How long does it take the ferry to cross the bay, Hightower ask." "Only about 30 minutes, Apollo answered." "What time do you expect us to get to the ferry dock?" "Once again, Apollo answered, we should be there 8:30 or 9 o'clock, anyway. It will be after dark." "That's good, Hightower said, that way a lot of the streets will be empty and we can make it to the jailhouse without running into too many people. Lewis, when we get on the other side and as we're getting off of the ferry I want you to make a beeline to the Sheriff's office and make sure he is awake and in his office so that we can get her into the jail and into a cell as quick as we possibly can. The fewer people that know she's in town, the better."

"Okay boss, that means that I need to be the last one on the ferry, so I can be the first one off." All of a sudden Apollo stopped and pointed to the north and said, "rider coming, and he's riding hard! Looks like Mason, Lewis said." Do you want me to ride out and meet him boss?"

"No, let's just wait right here for him." It wasn't long until they were sure that it was Mason Hightower, pulled out his 45 and fired it into the air. Having heard the gunshot Mason turned and looked and when he recognized the party he changed directions and headed directly for them. As he pulled up beside Hightower, he said, "sorry about taking so long boss, but little trees and I caught a couple of poachers hunting deer on the reservation without permission, so I arrested them and turned them over to the general." Then he threw up his hand with the palm facing Hightower and said, "don't worry boss, none of the women seen me turn these two men over, I was in and out in no time at all, I never seen any of the women, but there was plenty of troopers bivouacked completely around the ranch house. The only trooper that I spoke to was Sgt. Brown, and he chewed my ass out for riding the horse so hard, but when I told him why he saddled me a regular army mount and sent me on my way."

"How many deer did the poachers have Mason?" "They had two bucks and one large doe, we showed them to the general and he told Little Trees. There was no reason to let the meat go to waste. He ordered little trees to take the meat back to his people, compliments of the US Cavalry."

Hightower leaned his hat back and smiled right big and said, "that sounds like something the general would do. Did you find out if there had been any strangers around the ranch house, or stopping by the stockade for no reason?"

The general said everything was quiet and there had been no strangers or any kind of a disturbance in any way. He did say the ladies had busied theirselves by trying to finish the quilt that Mrs. Tatum was working on before she was killed. Oh, I almost forgot. Andrews, Rachel and Dorothy refused to let Katie leave, she's still there at the ranch house and I reckon the three ladies has developed quite a bond, it seems that they have been discussing wedding plans for Dorothy and Katie, or so the general says." Then Mason looked at Hightower and said, "as for Rachel and the babies their, fine. The dogs were lying on the front porch when I rode up, but they weren't there when I left the ladies must have let them back into the house, anyway boss, there's nothing for you to worry about, it would take a full company of troopers to get inside that house."

Resting his hands on the saddles horn, Hightower took a deep breath and said, "thanks for the informations Mason. Okay, Apollo, let's get to Lake Charles."!

Riding alongside Hightower, Mason looked at Elizabeth and said, "I see that she has still been running her mouth, or else she just likes to chew on that bandanna. You are going to burn that bandanna aren't you boss?"!!

"I might just burn not only the bandanna, but that saddle to!, I can't really picture anyone wanting to set in that saddle once they find out who was brought into town sittin on it.

The pace had quickened, they were now riding at a good gallop and the big gray's ears were standing straight up. There was the smell of saltwater in the air that told Hightower that they were getting really close to the bay. Hightower told Mason to ride ahead and make sure that the ferry was there, if it tries to leave, "hold it" we do not need to spend any time standing still. After all, we don't want to make Elizabeth a target."

"Andrews said, "boss you don't really expect anyone to try to kill her, do you?" "I really don't know what to expect. Andrews, but I was taught by a very smart law man years ago that not expecting the unexpected will get you killed, so yes, the way the people of Lake Charles felt about the judge and Army. I full expect that once the town finds out she is in the jail, they just might try tobreak her out and make her the center of attraction at a lynching party. The last thing that I want to do is have a confrontation with the people of Lake Charles over Elizabeth Carter, but I am charged by the law to protect her, not only from herself, but from anyone who would purposely do her bodily harm. You gentlemen might want to think about that yourself. As long as you wear those badges. On second thought get the saddlebags and Winchester's and bring them into the Sheriff's office and then take the horses to the stable, the pack horse too. Just in case there should be any gunplay the horses won't be in the line of fire, okay?"

Mason had taken off toward town at an easy gallop, much like a cowboy who was planning to make it a long evening in a saloon with a pretty waitress sittin on his lap. If luck was with them. The Sheriff would be in his office and maybe a deputy or two. As the men climbed back aboard their horses. Hightower looked at Elizabeth and said, I really do hope that you haven't been to uncomfortable Elizabeth, I surely do wish that this could have ended some other way, but I guess it just wasn't to be." With both of the lead rope's still on Elizabeth's mount the four men started into town at an easy walk. Everyone stayed as close to Elizabeth as they could. Hoping that no one would try to take a shot at her. When they were just about 200 yards away from the Sheriff's office Hightower seen Mason, the Sheriff, and two deputies step out onto the boardwalk. When they pulled up in front of the Sheriff's office. The Sheriff told his deputies, "get her off of that horse and get her inside."

The two deputies had already taken Elizabeth into the jailhouse. By the time everyone else, dismounted from their horses. Each man grabbed saddlebags and a Winchester and went into the Sheriff's office in less than a minute. Apollo and Andrews reappeared taking the reins of all the horses, and heading for the stables.

Once inside. Hightower asked the Sheriff, "do you have a woman that can come in here and search her for any kind of weapons, or anything like that. I want some blankets hung up in her cell for privacy, and I want a woman to strip search her, I want no stone left unturned." The Sheriff turned and looked at one of his deputies and told him, "go over to the saloon and get Caitlin and bring her back over here, don't answer any questions, just tell her it's important, now get."!

Hightower walked back to the cell where Elizabeth was, stepping inside the cell. Hightower pulled his knife and told her to turn around. He then took his knife and cut the rawhide strip that had been binding her wrist, stepping back outside and closing the cell door. He said, "as for the bandanna you keep it." There was a bombardment of foul language that came from Elizabeth, some of the words were even strange to Hightower, but he just let her rave."

The Sheriff looked over at Hightower and said, "she's a sassy one ain't she?" "Yep, she sure is, but make no mistake, she is also a cold blooded killer, and what makes it even worse is she enjoys killing. So don't you or your deputies in any way turn your back on her. As long as she is in this jail, Hightower said, I don't want her to have any visitors expect a lawyer, if she wants one. I mean it Sheriff, you check her meals, make sure that the only meals she gets is mostly sandwiches or something that she can drink, I don't want her to have any forks or spoons and absolutely not even a butter knife. Anytime anyone goes near that cell make sure that there is at least two people."

One of the deputies looked at Hightower and ask, "do you think any members of her gang will try to break her out Marshall?" "No, I don't believe they'll try anything like that, as far as I know they're all dead and buried way out in the Bayou, but keep alert and take nothing for granted, if you see something that doesn't seem right, It probably ain't, but don't check it out yourself, have someone with you."

The other deputy came through the front door with this lady by the arm, and he was trying to defend himself from her slapping and hitting him. The Sheriff raised his voice and said, "Caitlin, knock it off!. I just need you to do something for me and it has to be quiet, do you understand?" Caitlin shook her head yes, and then with a questioning look on her face she asked, "what is it you need from me that has to be so " Hush, Hush?" The Sheriff stood up and said, "follow me!"

Hightower stood watching as the lady pulled back the blanket and inside stood Elizabeth Stark naked, then came that crazy anointing laugh as she said, "I figured I'd save you a lot of trouble do you think I've got anything hid now, or would you like to check further.?" Caitlin picked up all of Elizabeth's clothes and went through them, piece by piece. There was nothing in her dress or in her blouse, but her corset was a different story. Caitlin found two sharpened metal spikes and one straight razor embedded where one of the splines in the corset was supposed to be, but is had been removed. Caitlin looked at Elizabeth, shook her head and said, "you're a naughty girl Ms. Carter. I guess you was planning on using this stuff to break out of jail. Sorry, but you'll have to get dressed without the corset. If you're hungry tell me what you want and I'll bring it over to you."

Elizabeth studied for a few moments and then said, "how about a couple of chicken legs and a couple of pieces of fresh bread and a big glass of sweet tea?" Caitlin looked at Elizabeth and said," I can bring you a couple of piece of chicken breast, but I can't bring you any chicken or any cut of meat at all if it has a bone in it. Other than that, would you like a fried dried Apple pie to go with that?" "I haven't had one of those in years, Elizabeth said. Yes, I believe I could handle one of them." Then Hightower heard Elizabeth say something he had never heard hear say, "thanks." Then she started putting her clothes back on, and Caitlin turned and stepped out of the cell carrying Elizabeth's corset, along with the two metal spikes and the straight razor.

The Sheriff escorted Caitlin back out to the main office and told her, "don't forget if she wants anything cut up, you cut I up, under no circumstances do you give her any kind of eating utensils. From what Hightower tells me about this woman. Even giving her a tin cup to drink coffee out of can be mighty dangers." "Caitlin said, you'd better ask her if she wants me to cut her chicken up for her, I didn't even think to ask her that. The deputy said." I'll ask her Sheriff", and he stepped back close to her cell and ask her. She was quick to answer no, she wanted to make sandwiches out of the chicken breast.

The deputy came back in and the Sheriff never gave him a chance to say anything, simply because Elizabeth had set it so loud that everyone in the outer office hear it, so the deputy ask the Sheriff if he needed him anymore tonight, if not, he was going home and get some shut eye.

"Go ahead and go home son, Hightower said, I'm going to be here tonight." Hightower picked up all of the Winchesters and unloaded them. He had finished cleaning the first Winchester when Apollo and Lewis came through the front door. Andrews had a worried look on his face. So Hightower ask him, what's wrong". "There's something going on down the Street at the saloon. There's a big meeting going on for some reason, and it's not only men, there's a lot of women also."

Hightower got up and walked over to the wall and took down three shotgun, he handed one to Andrews, one to Lewis, and one to Mason. Apollo stood there with his hand out and said, "I will stand beside you, the judge would have liked that." "Turning to the Sheriff Hightower said, "swear him in, and give him a badge. Mason, you didn't ride in with us, so I want you to take your badge off, go down to the livery stable get your horse and ride down to the saloon and get yourself a beer. Mason looked at Hightower questionably and ask, "why can't I just walked down?" "Because you need to look like a cowboy, just coming into town for a cold beer."

Apollo spoke up and said, "if anyone asked who you're working for, just tell them, Poppa John's son, Maurice. Everybody know Poppa John." Without asking another question Mason went out the back door and made his way to the stables and took Apollo's horse, simply because it had his family's brand on it. He couldn't very well ride his horse down there in front of the saloon with a United States cavalry brand, and tell him he was working on a ranch just a little ways out of town. Mason thought to himself, "I seem to be getting a little smarter, maybe I need to hang around Hightower a little longer."

Getting on his horse before he left the stable. He rode out into the street and directly up to the saloon where he had to actually make people move so he could get to the hitching rail. Then as he got down he saw one of the men look at the brand on the horse and evidently it was enough to convince him that the rider of this horse was okay because he turned away and went back to talking. As Mason was tying his horse to the hitching rail. He asked, "what the hell is going on around here, are they havein some kind of an election or something?"

One short heavy set man said, "somebody just brought word that Ed Hightower has brought in that crazy bitch, that murdered judge Tatum and his wife Amy. And these people are planning on getting her out of that jail and stringing her up to that big oak tree on the north side of town. I reckon as soon as they feel they've had enough to drink, they'll go drown there and take her.

Mason, tipped his hat back and said, "Mr. I don't know about that, I've been told that that Hightower Feller don't back down from nothing. I've even heard it said that when the governor needs a Marshall that has no qualms about killing He called's on this Hightower."

"I really don't think when he sees the amount of people coming down the street that he'll try to stand up to them. He's got to be smarter than that." Mason just shook his head and started walking, all the time saying, "well, it ain't nothing to me, but I'm not going up against him, I like living too much.". Then he stopped and asked the heavyset man, "do you think there's going to be some shooting? If you do, maybe I better get my horse down to the livery stable and out of the way." "That just might be a good idea young Feller," a tall, bearded man said as he was checking his 45.

Mason didn't hesitate any longer. He turned around, untied Apollo's horse from the hitching rail, mounted it and headed for the stable. Riding the horse right into the stables, he loosened the cinch and put the horse away. Then he headed out the back door around the back of the buildings and as he peeked around the corner of the Sheriff's office he could see that no one was paying attention, so he casually stepped up on the boardwalk took about four large steps and slid into the Sheriff's office.

Hightower looked up and said, "what did you find out Mason?" "I found out there are a bunch of pissed off people up there at that saloon, and their drinking whiskey and talkin about coming down here and taken Elizabeth and inviting her to a lynching party, and boss every one of them is carrying some kind of a weapon. I got a funny feeling that there's going to be plenty of dead people lying in the middle of that street before this is over with."

"Lewis, go over there by the window and get in a position where you can see up the street and keep an eye on them People, let me know when they start this way. Sheriff if you will, I would like for you and your two deputies to step back in the cell section. Don't let Elizabeth take those blankets down they need to be up just in case somebody tries to shoot through one of those windows back there. The rest of you men check your shotguns and your 45s. And don't come out on the boardwalk until I tell you to."

"What are you going to do boss? Andrews ask. "I'm going to try something stupid, I'm going to try and talk some sense to these people, remember don't show yourselves until I say the word "deputies".

Without saying anything more. Hightower opened the front door and stepped out onto the boardwalk closing the door behind him. He then pulled him up a chair and leaned up against the front of the Sheriff's office and propped his feet up on to a post, and waited.

He could tell they were getting pretty close to being liquored up enough to make their play, simply because of how loud they were getting. He knew they could see him on the front porch of the Sheriff's office and he had tried his best to get an approximate headcount of how many people there were. The best he could figure was about60, and growing all the time.

Finally a gentleman stepped out of the saloon carrying a rope and a Winchester and said to the rest of the people, "I've waited long enough, it's time for this party to start." Hightower could tell that this man was no stranger to lynchings, or to violence. Then man was wearing a 45 hung low and tied down. This meant to Hightower, that the man was one of two things, and outlaw wanting to build a name, or a gunfighter also wanting to build himself a name. Like a man on a mission, the stranger led the whole saloon full of people down the street and when they got within 10 feet of the jail, Hightower said, "that's far enough."

"You people need to go home, and you need to do it now. What you people are planning to do, or try I should say, is only going to get a lot of people hurt and some killed. Before you go any further would some of your mind answering a couple of questions for me?" The man carrying the rope told Hightower to go ahead and ask his questions. So he did.

"How many of you people actually knew the judge and his wife?" Quite a few of the people help up their hands. "How many of you people respected the judge and his wife?" Almost everyone held their hand up, and then Hightower ask the final question, "do you really think that the judge would approve of what you're doing, or would he stand out here on this boardwalk and point his finger at you and tell you in no uncertain terms to " take your drunk ass's back home."! "You are the people that judge Tatum stood up for, and fought for every day of his life. And your first act of honoring him is to do something that you know absolutely the judge would never stand for. What kind of friends are you? To honor the man you want to break the very thing that he stood for, "the law". I am prepared to die right here on this boardwalk, if that's what it takes to stop you from doing this, then that's how it's going to be.

Then Hightower looked at the man carrying the rope and said, "Mr. you come before me with a tied down 45 and the smell of whiskey on your breath. Now I'm going to tell you something, and I'm only going to say it once. You touch that 45 and I'll kill you, and to answer the question that's in your eyes, yes Sir, I'm that fast. The rest of you if you care anything at all about the judge and his wife, you'll honor him and her by clearing the streets, "now."

After making that statement Hightower stood up and very slowly stepped over in front of the door of the jailhouse and turned facing the man carrying the rope and looking him directly in the eye. He said, "put the rope down, turn around and walk away. Mr., and I won't ask again." The man laid the rope down, walked backwards, never taking his eyes off of Hightower, until he was about 20 feet away, then he stopped and said, "I ain't never backed down from a fight, and I ain't going to start today.

His colt was only about halfway out its holster. When Hightower's bullet struck him in the center of his chest, the man staggered and with a look on his face of utter disbelief, he dropped to his knees and then fell flat on his face in the dust of main Street. Hightower then said, "that man did not have to die, neither do you. Now go home folks, and let the law take care of Elizabeth Carter. Make the judge proud, do the right thing."

As the people started to mill around and empty the Street, Hightower pointed at four men and said, "you stood behind him. When he held the rope, now you four men pick him up and take him to the undertaker's." The four men without saying a word, picked up the stranger and preceded to carry him across the Street to the funeral parlor.

As the people dispersed, the front door of the jailhouse opened and stepping out onto the boardwalk led by Apollo was Mason, Lewis, and Andrews. Mason looked over at Hightower with a smile and said, "man, am I glad I'm on your side."

Hightower, without looking at Mason, or any of the other deputies simply said, "me too." Apollo handed Hightower his shotgun, shook Hightower's hand and said, "it's time for me to get back to the Bayou, I don't want to be deputy anymore." Taking the badge off of his chest, Apollo, kissed it, and said, "for you judge, I have wore this badge to help set things right, now I go home with peace in my heart."

Hightower watched Apollo as he walked down the boardwalk and into the stables and within a couple of minutes. He walked his horse out and then swung into the saddle. Taking his hat off and waving it in the air, he said, "Hightower, you, like the general are my friend." He then turned his horse South, headed back to the ferry and home.

The Sheriff came walking out from the cell section of his jail and said, "Hightower, I got to hand it to you, you saved a lot of lives today." "Not really Sheriff, these people are good people, and like everyone, when you lose a friend. It affects you in strange ways.

"Sheriff, I think you and your deputies can handle it from here on, I think it's time that the four of us got back to normal life. If you need me or us, just have someone go to the telegraph office and send the wire to the stockade in Turner Texas care of general Whitehead, and we'll get the message." Mason butted in and said, "boss, do you think we can get some breakfast before we head back to the ranch, I surely hate for them. Women have to cook for us, when it ain't eaten time."

Hightower studied for just a moment and then shaking his head yes he said, "I don't see why we can't have some breakfast, besides it's going to give us a chance to see Lewis's lady friend."

Andrews jumped up and told Mason, "come on, Mason you and I'll go get the horses, that'll give the boss and Lewis a chance to get over to the restaurant and get a table, besides all four of us going in there at the same time might scare her to death."

Hightower stood at the front of the Sheriff's office and watched the two young men, and he could see in their actions the air of new found energy and freedom to act like the young men they were for a change. They were laughing and joking, as they headed for the stables. It then finally dawned on Hightower that the ordeal of chasing down Elizabeth Carter and her outlaw friends had come to an end. The only thing left was for Elizabeth to stand trial for the murder of two very fine people.

As he and Lewis started across the street a buckboard came down the main Street with two ponies pulling it at a hard gallop. Holding on to the reins was Rachel Hightower, along with her was Dorothy, and Katie, and two children. Rachel pulled up and jumped form the buckboard and ran over to Hightower and smacked him right across the face, then she grabbed him and hugged him and said, "that was for not letting me know that you had made it to Lake Charles, and that you were safe, don't ever do that to me again Edward Hightower.

Lewis spoke up and said, Mrs. Hightower, we were just about to have us some breakfast before heading back to the ranch, would you and Dorothy and Katie consider joining us? Besides, there's someone I want you to meet."

"Oh, that's right, Lewis your lady friend works here, we would be proud to meet her," then Dorothy spoke up, "sure, we'll join you. I don't know about anybody else but I'd like to have a breakfast that I didn't have to cook or at least help cook."

Then there was on outburst of laughter from the ladies as Hightower took the tether line and tied the buckboard to a hitching rail. Almost at the same time. Andrews and Mason Road up leading Mason's horse and Comanche. Jumping down from their horses, they tied them to the other hitching rail and then preceded to say hello to their two young ladies by grabbing them in a breath Stopping hug and then a kiss. Then, Hightower said, "if you four young lovers don't mind I would sure like to get me some breakfast, you can do as much of that later, as you want to, unless the general has something for you three to do. Which, if I don't get some breakfast, I just might ask him to find something for you to spend some energy on." This made everybody laugh even harder.

Everyone sat down at a long table and the waitress that came over to wait on them was a really pretty young lady and by the actions of Lewis, she was, the mystery lady, so everyone just sat tight and waited for Lewis to introduce her. Finally, Lewis stood up and said, folks, I want you to meet the love of my life, this is Eve Mendelson and I have asked her to be my wife and she has most graciously accepted. Eve, honey this is Edward and Rachel Hightower, and her sister Dorothy and her soon to be husband Mr. Mason, over here sets Kate Bitterman and her soon to be husband Mr. Andrews, now that everyone has met every body can we please set down and have some breakfast.

Eve spoke up and said, "I'll make it easy on everyone we have an extremely good special today, it's a simple breakfast, bacon, eggs, biscuits and gravy for a dollar and a quarter. If you want this all I need to know is how you want your eggs,?" Everyone said at the same time, "over medium." Eve laughed and said", you folks even talk like a tight knit family."

"Oh, we are a tightknit family Eve, Rachel said, whenever one of the men gets in trouble, they're all In trouble. So we ladies have got to stick together and hold our ground, because the more you know these four, the more you will understand. They are constantly getting into something, but they always seem to understand how to get out of it."

"When we get done eating breakfast, Hightower said, I'm going home and go to bed and I am going to sleep for as long as I possibly can. I'm not even so sure that I'll come back in town for Elizabeth trial, or anything else for at least a week."

That's when a voice came from behind him, saying, "I'm sorry to tell you this Marshall, but you will be required at mrs Carter's trial, you will be required to testify because you are the arresting officer."

Hightower looked at the elderly gentleman sitting at the table and said, "who are you the prosecutor?" "No, Sir, I'm federal judge Jim Ebsen, the new federal judge appointed to take over judge Tatum's courtroom, these are the orders of the governor of the state of Louisiana. Please believe me when I say I did not asked for this post, no judge would want to set on the bench in the shadow of judge Tatum. He was an outstanding judge and an even better human being. I can't speak for everyone in the capital but as far as I am concerned, he will be extremely missed."

"When do you expect the trial to start."? "With what I've seen so far from the townspeople, the sooner the trial is started, the better. So she will be arraigned at 9o'clock in the morning and a lawyer will be appointed for her then. You won't be expected at the arraignment, but you will be expected here at 8 AM day after tomorrow for the start of the trial."

Hightower looked at the judge and said", you do realize that Elizabeth is my stepmother, and the judge and his wife Amy are my father and mother-in-law. By all rights judge, I should not have to testify on anything other than what I had to go through to bring her in. I was not present when the judge and Amy were killed, as far as everything goes these three deputies could testify just to keep it on the up and up, and you could disqualify me because of my ties to both parties. Why don't you think about that judge,? I spent two years chasing this woman, I want no further part of what happens to her."

The judge said, "just the same Marshall, I will expect you in court 8 AM day after tomorrow, don't be late." When he turned around. Rachel was looking at him and all Hightower could think to say was "sounds a lot like your father, don't he."

After that there was nothing much going on, except a lot of laughter and telling stories on each other. Andrews told of how much Apollo helped in the capture, and also the protection of Elizabeth. He told of how the man had led the posse into the Bayou and had led us, so quietly that the four men were able to surround the gang. He also told of how they went down fighting, and then he told of how Hightower had snuck into the camp and found Elizabeth and had killed her personal security man,, and knocked her out at the same time in order to take her alive.

Mason told how much Little Trees contributed to the capture of Mrs. Carter. Mason also told us how he had led them and read the sign that brought them to the place where they entered the Bayou, and he told of how the young Indian had stood guard and watched over them, and how well that he and Apollo worked together. Then he told of how much Apollo and his brother thought of the judge and Amy.

Hightower set there, very quiet and pretty soon. Rachel recognized how quiet he was, and she ask, "Edward, you've got something on your mind, tell me what it is!" "I don't know Rachel, I just got a gut feeling that the worst is not over, maybe I'm just being paranoid, but I can't seem to erase that feeling. I really should stay in town tonight and help the Sheriff and his deputies, but I need to go home to spend time with my wife and my kids. I just can't bring myself to allow her any possibility of escaping again."

Lewis spoke up and said, "boss, I was kind of planning to stay in town tonight, anyway. So if it's all right with you, I can sack out at the jailhouse tonight. That should give you the peace of mind to go home and sleep in your own bed tonight. If you need to come back, then come back tomorrow and check everything out, fair enough?"

Rachel spoke up and said, "Mr. Lewis, that sounds like an excellent idea to me, what do you think about that miss Mendelson? "It's fine with me, it'll give me a little time to spend with him and I still won't be interfering with his job."

Hightower spoke up, "Andrews, Lewis, Mason, I'm really sorry that I have been so hard on you. You three have done an excellent job, not only with putting up with me, but doing honor to the badge that you wear. I must confess, so I have been sorely tempted to give up my badge and spend time with my wife and my children on our ranch, but my wife so expertly pointed out that being a law man was what I am. I was a law man when she met me, and I guess I'll be a law man the day that I die. She says she can live with me wearing this badge, and she doesn't believe that I can live without it it's too much a part of me. So gentlemen, if I ever need you again consider your self always my deputies, and I am looking forward to the day when the three of you take your wedding vows in the backyard at our ranch, and as a wedding gift. I was prepared and still am to build three houses. One for the Andrews, one for the Lewis's, and one for the Masons. That is a wedding gift to each of you from my wife and myself. As far as I am concerned from this day on, "your family.".

After breakfast was over, Rachel, Dorothy and Katie climb back aboard the buckboard and the last thing Rachel said, was "I'll be waiting at the house for you." Hightower felt that he needed to go by the jailhouse one more time, he just couldn't get used to the idea that the ordeal with Elizabeth Carter was over. He wanted for his own satisfaction to see Elizabeth behind bars just to ensure that he's not dreaming and beside he needed to know what caused her to turn to killing.

As he stood watching the buckboard go out of town. Hightower felt a gnawing in his stomach that he couldn't explain. He had untied Comanche, and was leading him down the street toward the Sheriff's office. When he noticed two horses tied in between the Sheriff's office and the general store.

Stopping two doors down. He tied Comanche, and then he took a good long look at the two horses, and realized the two horses had the brand of the ranch that Elizabeth had bought under the same of Lily Barnes in New Mexico. Setting down in the shadows Hightower drew his 45 and waited. No more than five minutes had passed when a cowboy came out of the Sheriff's office with another man, but Hightower realized it was not a man, it was Elizabeth. Just as they were about to reach the horses. Hightower stepped out of the shadows and said, "there won't be any escape this time." The young cowboy turned with his 45 already in his hand and the two men fired at exactly the same time. Hightower felt the young Cowboy's bullet dig deep into his shoulder, but the young cowboy never realized that he had hit Hightower, because the light in his eyes was out. When he hit the ground. Elizabeth tried to mount the horse, but Hightower caught her, and slung her to the ground, pointing his 45 at her, he said, "not this time. Elizabeth, get up." Taking Elizabeth by the arm. Hightower led her back into the Sheriff's office and back into the cell section where he found the Sheriff and his deputy bound hand and foot, and gagged in the cell where is Elizabeth had been. After forcing Elizabeth down on the floor face down, he took out his knife and cut the Sheriff's hand's loose and then handed him the knife so he could release his feet and then released the deputy.

The Sheriff immediately told his deputy, "you go find the Fellers that came in with him and get them over here now." The Sheriff and Hightower stepped out of the cell and after locking the door the Sheriff turned to Hightower and said," Marshall your bleeding pretty bad, can you make it to the doctors office?" I don't think so Sheriff." Having become quite dizzy Hightower felt a blanket of black falling over him.

When he opened his eyes. It took a few minutes for Hightower to realize where he was, the Sheriff had managed to get him to the doctors office and the Dr. had done surgery on Hightower's shoulder and he was bound up as the Dr. had taped his left arm to his chest. After dressing his wound. The loss of blood had caused Hightower to pass out, but the deputy had done his job, it was Lewis and Andrew that had carried him from the Sheriff's office to the doc's. The first thing Hightower ask was, "where's Carter,"?

The Sheriff spoke up and said," right now she's back in her cell with three armed deputies watching her, and two more deputies in the main office. Because of her attempted escape the judge arraigned her right in her cell and instead of the arraignment being tomorrow morning, her trial will start tomorrow morning, the way she is ranting and raving the judge heard her in her own voice confess to the killings numerous people, including the judge and his wife, and vowing that if she can get out that jail. She will do her best to kill every person in the city of Lake Charles.

The Sheriff scratched his head and said, "she said the damnedest thing, she is bound and determined that if she hangs, she wants to be hung by the same rope that hung her son." Then the Sheriff looked at Hightower and said, "you know that I'm a new elected Sheriff. I don't know what she's talking about, do you Marshall?" "I sure do, Hightower said, I know you've heard of Raymond Carter," "yes Sir, I have heard the name the Sheriff said." "Well, Raymond Carter were her son, and I'm the one who brought him in. The thing that makes everything so dam sticky is Raymond was my half brother and Elizabeth Carter was my stepmother. My father left her many years ago, and I guess it, set her off because she married another man named Kershaw, who had two sons of his own. She murdered him and made outlaws out of his two sons and eventually the two deputies that used to work here shot one of them down after he took a shot at me and missed that he hit my wife. All this happened well before Rachel gave birth to the twins. Elizabeth Carter has blamed me and my father for everything that's happened to her and she is so eat up with hate that I don't think she really knows why she killed people, she just needs to strike out at something. I think that every person she killed in her mind was either me or my father."

Eve Mendelson was sitting next to the bed and she leaned over and touched Hightower's arm and said, "Alan is on his way to catch Rachel and Dorothy, he felt they should know about Elizabeth attempted escape and you're being wounded."

Hightower raised his right hand and placed it against his head and said, "oh boy, all hell is going to break loose Now, she is going to be pissed. Sheriff, Hightower said, don't let her anywhere near that jail, she's just apt to shoot Elizabeth Carter, and I'm not joking."!!!

Then he looked back at Eve and told her, "you tell Lewis to take Rachel back to the ranch and between him and Mason make sure she stays there, can you do that for me, miss Mendelson?" "Yes Sir, I most certainly can."

Without saying another word Eve was out of her chair and out the door, Almost at a dead run. The doctors wife pulled the cover up over Hightower's chest and said in a very Stern voice, "you know the drill Mr. Hightower, go to sleep and get some rest, or by jingles I'll give you something that will knock you out,"

Knowing that the docs wife did not beat around the bush and would not pull any punches, Hightower leaned back and laid his head on a very firm pillow and it was as though his body was saying," okay son, we've had about all we can stand for a while, I'm going to shut down for a while." Hightower could feel the peacefulness of sleep. Slowly spreading over his body and for the first time in a long time he felt at ease.

Eve Mendelson was standing in front of the doctors office. When Lewis brought Rachel and Dorothy back in the buckboard. She stopped Rachel from getting down from the buckboard by saying, "Mrs. Hightower, I've got a message for you from your husband. He's okay. He's resting right now, and he told me to tell you to go back to the ranch," then she looked at Lewis and said,"his orders to you, Alan is you and Mason are to take these two back to the ranch and make damn sure they stay there, even if you have to hogtie them. The way he said it, I really don't believe I would try to go against that order." Rachel finally spoke up and said, "just how bad was he wounded?" "It's his left shoulder, from what I understand it's the same shoulder that the arrowhead was removed from. This time he was lucky the bullet was a through and through. The Dr. has already stitched him up and dressed his wound, he has also been given something to make him sleep so he asked me to deliver this message to you, Rachel and he said, make sure you go home.".

Lewis could see the anger welling up in Rachel's face and she started to get down from the buckboard, but he stopped her by saying, "Rachel, the boss wouldn't have said what he did. If he hadn't meant it, and I know you don't want to hear this but he gave me an order and ma'am, I'm not going against the boss in any way. So you stay right there in that buckboard." Then Rachel ask, "well, can I at least go to the jail and see this woman?" "No ma'am, Eve said, the Sheriff has strict orders from your husband, he is not to let you anywhere near that jail and he meant it when he said it because he's afraid you might try to shoot Elizabeth Carter and as he put it, "that ain't gonna happen."!!!......

There, she reluctantly, Rachel turned the buckboard around and with Lewis and Mason on their horses, and right behind them. They headed for the ranch. Dorothy and Katie each had a child in their arms and Dorothy said, "it's for the best Rachel. The babies need fed and they need to be put down for their nap, Katie needs to get home and we need to brief the general on what has happened.

"If he doesn't start taking better care of himself, and stop taking these chances, I swear I'm going to shoot him, myself." Rachel said. Dorothy laughed and said, "you might shoot someone else, but Rachel, you're just blowing smoke whenever you say that you would do any kind of harm to Edward Hightower, you very well could love him to death, but you would never harm him in any way. You know that and so do I."

"I know, but sometimes he makes me so damn mad. He believes in his job so much, and he takes pride in doing his job right, but in order to do his job. He must take chances and that's the part of the job I don't like." "Look at it like this Rachel, Dorothy said, as soon as he's able to come home, you're going to have him there for at least two weeks while he heals up, so you can take care of him or you can make his life miserable for that two weeks, or you can love him and show him the same strength that he has showed you, so many times. Besides, after being round the house for a couple of weeks being taken care of by you he'd just may get used to the idea and want to stay around permanently., Katie added, I know if Kenneth was to ever get hurt. I would baby him so much that he would never want to leave."

Dorothy spoke up and said, "if he didn't want to leave. How would he make money to buy food, what would you live on?" Katie laughed real loud and said", we'd live on love, honey, lots of love."!!!!!!

When they arrived at the ranch, Lewis and Mason seen the general in the compound and rode up to him. Without dismounting they explained the situation to the general, not only about Hightower, but about the two women. The General just nodded his head and said, "tell Hightower, not to worry, I'll take care of it. As for you two get back to town and take care of business. Swinging their horses around the men headed back toward

Lake Charles at a hard gallop. There was only one thing on the two deputies minds. This thing with Elizabeth Carter had to end and end now.

The Dr. sedated Hightower for the rest of that day and then allowed him to sleep naturally that night. Awakening early the next morning, Hightower set up on the side of the bed and decided to test his legs and see if he could stand. Taking his time he stood for just a few moments and then sat back down. He sat on the edge of the bed for about five minutes and then he stood up again. This time he remained standing for around five minutes, not wanting to push it too hard, he sat back down. He was about to stand up for the third time when the Dr. came in and when he seen Hightower setting up on the edge of the bed he ask, "are you feeling well enough really to be setting up?" "Hell doc, I was just about to stand up for the third time, how about given me a hand?"

The doctor walked over and took Hightower by his right arm and helped him stand. Hightower in turn walked very slowly over to the window and looked out at the main Street of town. Never taking his eyes off of Main St., Hightower ask the doctor, "have they started Elizabeth trial yet?" "They're just about to, do you think you can make it?" The Dr. ask that because he knew that Hightower was going to go to that trial, he had to for his own peace of mind.

I'm glad to see that I still have my pants on, and my socks. So if you'll help me get my boots and my shirt on. Maybe you can find somebody to get me to the courthouse, or at least walk along with me." "Two of your deputies are setting outside right now, I believe their names are, Lewis and Mason. I'm quite sure they'll be more than happy to get you to the courthouse."

The doctor left the room and in very short order Lewis and Mason walked in to the room and it was Mason that spoke up saying, "what ever you need boss, we're here to do it." "Then get me to the courthouse, Hightower said, but first help me get my shirt on."

Taking their time and allowing Hightower to stop occasionally, they accompanied him all the way to the courthouse. The trial was just about start when the three men entered the courtroom. The judge looked at Hightower over the top of his glasses and said, I wasn't so sure that you were going to be able to make it Marshall." "Well, from the way you talked at the restaurant. I figured if I didn't I'd end up in jail and, from the way your attitude was you just might have put me in the same cell with Mrs. Carter." Setting down on the first pew, Hightower noticed a slight smile on the judge's face. He then said, "I was going to notify you Marshall that Elizabeth Carter has confessed to the killing of the Hon. Judge Walter Tatum and his wife Amy, and for the sake of all she has pled guilty, so we really don't need any testimony from you Marshall, if you want to you can leave." No, Sir, I need to hear it for myself that this is over."

The judge pounded his gavel and the Sheriff jumped up and said, "okay, everybody settle down this Court's in session." The judge looking very solemn, looked at Elizabeth Carter and told her to stand up. Then he said, "Elizabeth Carter you are already under the sentence of life in prison for the murders of your ex husband, the high Sheriff of Las Cruces, New Mexico and the murders of the two deputies that were transporting you to prison. If it weren't for the fact that since you escaped you have been responsible through bank robberies and personal vendettas the killing of at least three more people. But you made a mistake young lady when you killed a federal judge and his wife. The mandatory sentence for the death of a federal judge is death by hanging. So here with your confession of the murders of Walter and Amy Tatum, I have no recourse but to sentence you to be hanged by the neck until dead, one week from today. Until then, you will be held under guard by the office of the Sheriff of Lake Charles Louisiana until the day of your execution. Then up on that day you will be escorted to the gallows by United states Marshall Edward Hightower. May God have mercy on your soul." Then after staring at Ms. Carter for just a few moments he ask," do you have anything that you would like to say?"

Elizabeth stood up and with her last ounce of strength and every ounce of resentment and hate that she could produce she said, "to hell with a whole bunch of you, you had better kill me this time or this whole town will pay. Especially you. Edward Hightower, I will kill you, that sassy little wife you've got, and then I'll pick up your babies and spread their brains on the nearest big rock that I can find." With that the Sheriff grabbed her by the arms and him, Lewis, Mason, and Andrews escorted her out of the courthouse, accross the street to the jail and even when she was locked up. She was still ranting and raving about killing as many people as she possibly could. As Hightower walked out of the courtroom onto the courthouse steps, he was met by Rachel and without saying a word, or asking for any help two citizens helped Hightower on to the buckboard and then only then did Rachel speak "well, Mr. Hightower, are you ready to go home now?"

Suddenly Hightower felt very tired and he looked over at Rachel and with a smile of contentment, he said, "yes ma'am, and if I try to leave anytime within the next month, would you be so kind as to shoot me in the ass."

"I can't do that, Rachel said, because there are two young ladies waiting at the ranch that you have been given the responsibility of walking them down the aisle and giving them away at their wedding, which will be performed in our backyard three weeks from today.

"Rachel, I never did find out why she took to killin, but I guess it really doesn't matter anymore, does it?" "No, it doesn't Rachel said with a smile, and thank the good Lord above in one week. It will be over with completely. And until then, Mr. Hightower, I have been instructed by the Dr. not to let you do any thing strenuous, I told him that I would do my best to see it that you stayed in bed for the entire week." Then she smiled and giggled at Hightower and set the two ponies into a gallop in the direction of the Hightower ranch.

The next six days went by very fast for Hightower and his family, they spent a lot of time setting on the front porch with Junior and Rebecca playing on a blanket and being guarded by King and Josie. Where tension once reigned now you heard only laughter and talk of what needed to be done on the ranch. Such as fixing fence, separating the calfs from their mothers so they could be branded with the circle H brand. And of course there was plans being drawn up for the building of three more houses and the women spent most of their time planning for the wedding. General Whitehead acted as if he was the father of all three of the young ladies that were to be married. Hightower noticed for the first time since he had known the general, that the general could smile every once in a while. It was plain to see that Dorothy, Katie and Eve had him wrapped right around their little fingers. Whether the general wanted to admit it or not, he was enjoying every minute of it.

Then the morning of the seventh day, Rachel had gotten up early and had laid out some clean clothes for Hightower to wear. She had also shined his boots and sat them at the edge of the bed where he would get to them.

The nights before she had helped him take a bath and shaved him with the skill of a license Barber. Then she awakened Hightower and said "it's time to get up, today is the day. Elizabeth is scheduled to pay for her crimes and all the bad things she has done in the past two years, everything she's responsible for goes away today. After today we will no longer live in fear of being shot from ambush."

Hightower got up from the bed stood for just a minute, then he reached and took his arm out of the sing where he had carried it for one solid week. Looking at Rachel. While he straightened his left arm and moved it slowly to try to relive the stiffness he said, "I will not go into town looking as if I am hurt, I want her to see that she failed to hurt me physically." Then with a determination he got dressed, but found very quickly that he needed help with his boots. Walking out of the bedroom and into the kitchen, he picked up his gun belt and with Rachel's help strapped it on. She had already penned the badge on his vest so when she slipped it on him. He was fully dressed except for his hat.

Rachel told him to set down and she would fix him a cup of coffee, and ask him if he wanted some breakfast? Hightower simply said, "no, sweetheart, I've got enough time to drink one cup of coffee while I'm drinking that cup of coffee. Can you send one of the sentries down to find my three deputies? There a part of this too, and they need to see it through to the finish. It needs to be something that they will never forget. Hanging a woman doesn't happen every day." Stepping out the back door. Rachel asked the Sentry to go find the three deputies, and she was quickly told that they were on the front porch waiting for the Marshall.

When Hightower heard what the Sentry said he turned up his cup of coffee and downed it, kissed Rachel and said, "I'll be back when it's over," then he left the kitchen and without any pause stepped on to the front porch. There were four horses saddled and tied to the hitching rail, all Hightower said was, "let's get this cover with." Without a word, the four men stepped up on their horses, and rode out of the compound that a hard gallop, headed for Lake Charles, to witness the last day in Elizabeth Carter's life.

When the four men rode up in front of the Sheriff's office. They were met not only by the Sheriff, but by the judge. After dismounting Hightower shook hands with the judge and the Sheriff and said, "I know I cut it close,

I just didn't want to spend any more time then I had too with Elizabeth, is she ready to go Sheriff?" "Marshall personally I think she's looking forward to it, so yes, she's ready."

The Sheriff walked back into the jail and very shortly, he brought Elizabeth out, she was handcuffed and she was dressed in a very nice dress, her hair was brushed and had ribbons tied holding two ponytails. As she come out of the Sheriff's office. She stopped and looked at Hightower for a minute or so and then she said in a very matter of fact way, "let's go."

The Sheriff had a gallows built behind the jailhouse and it seemed that everyone in town was surrounding it. But for some reason it was deathly quiet. The only sound to be heard was the occasional cry of a baby. Without any pause at all Elizabeth walked up the 13 steps and stood directly under the noose with her head held high and her eyes staring off in the distance focused on something far away. When asked if she had any last words, all Elizabeth did was shake her head. "no ,". Then a hood was placed over her head and the rope around her neck.

With everything in place Hightower stepped up really close to Elizabeth and whispered in her ear, "May God have mercy on you Elizabeth" he then stepped back, looked at the Sheriff and nodded his head. The silence was broken by the sound of the trap door as it opened and dropped Elizabeth.

It was so quiet that when the noose tightened around Elizabeth's neck, when it reached the end of its length, There was a loud "snap" as Elizabeth's neck broke.

With out looking back, Hightower walked back down the 13 steps straight over to Comanche, stepped into the saddle and at an easy gallop, he rode away, leaving behind him. The remains of a very evil woman.

www.ingramcontent.com/pod-product-compliance
Lightning Source LLC
LaVergne TN
LVHW091555060526
838200LV00036B/845